Pray For a Miracle

Pray For a Miracle

MICHALEI SCHAAN

Published by Tate Publishing & Enterprises, LLC
127 E. Trade Center Terrace | Mustang, Oklahoma 73064 USA
1.888.361.9473 | www.tatepublishing.com

Tate Publishing is committed to excellence in the publishing industry. The company reflects the philosophy established by the founders, based on Psalm 68:11,
"The Lord gave the word and great was the company of those who published it."

Cover design by Jan Sunday Quilaquil
Interior design by Caypeeline Casas

Published in the United States of America

ISBN: 978-1-62746-627-1
1. Fiction / General
2. Fiction / Christian / General
13.10.01

Dedication

To my sweet sister, Kaitlyn, who supported me each step of the way. I love you so much! God has made you so beautiful, and I am lucky to have you as my best friend and sister. You are my angel!

To Jesus who gave me the words to write—they are not my own, but from you, O God. You are my inspiration, and my prayer is that my life is not glorifying to me but to you. My life is not my own; my life is yours.

To Jesus Christ who loves us and released us from our sins by His blood—and He has made us to be a kingdom, priests to His God and Father—to Him be the glory and dominion forever and ever. Amen.

Revelation 1:5–6 (NASB)

Acknowledgments

My dear, precious Savior, Jesus Christ, you are my inspiration, and I thank you for continuously walking beside me. Although I do not deserve your amazing love, you still extend your grace to me. I fail over and over again; I am self-conscious instead of God-conscious. May you continuously work in my heart and change me for your glory, not my own. Let your breath of life that you breathed into me be evident daily as you live through me. I want this to be my steadfast desire, "But as for me and my house, we will serve the Lord" (Joshua 24:15, NASB). Thank you for helping me through every winding path in my life. Your love and compassion never fail. I love you, Jesus.

My remarkable parents, you have been there for me through every storm that crashes into my life. Thank you for sharing your wisdom. Without you, I would not have had the privilege of knowing Jesus Christ as my personal Savior. Over the years, I have learned that parents are a treasure from God, and I often find that I take you for granted. You are truly precious to me, and I thank God that He chose me to be your daughter. I love you, Mom and Dad.

My beautiful sisters, although we are growing up and we are nearing a crossroad where our lives will separate, I will always cherish you dearly. I pray that God will unveil his destiny to each of you and that he will use you in the unique way he has designed you for. I love you, my dear sisters.

Contents

Forgiveness

The morning was cool with a misty fog outlining the vast breezes of the air. As Charlene opened her stiff, green eyes, she stared blankly at the room surrounding her. She remembered everything now; it was beginning to seem so clear. Last night, her husband Todd was driving, and a drunk driver had collided head-on into his lane. Her husband had tried to avoid the collision, but there was no way of escaping it. Now, he was at the hospital suffering a coma. Doctors weren't sure if he would survive the accident because it was so severe. Charlene just kept praying that Todd would come through alive. She had never told him her secret, and how she longed she had. If he never woke up, she would blame herself continuously for hiding her secret from him. Sitting in the chair next to his bed, she slowly folded her hands. Praying softly, Charlene cried out her heart to God.

"Why, God? Why? What are you doing to me? You've taken away my first husband, Nate, and now, you are taking away Todd right before my eyes. You've taken away Todd's parents. I don't understand. Why? What have I done to deserve all of this?"

"Are you all right, ma'am?" a nurse kindly asked as she stepped into the tranquil room. The heavier set woman was wearing a straight, white uniform with her white hair pulled back into a smooth, tight bun.

Charlene nodded as she firmly gripped Todd's sturdy hand. The nurse whispered softly, "Why don't you come downstairs to the café and get something to eat. I think you'll feel much better." Charlene just glared at her, her thoughts spinning through her head. If only she could hear Todd's soothing voice, everything would be fine. If only she had told him her secret that she was pregnant. Why had she waited to tell him? Now, he may never know. Oh, how she wished that man in the other car didn't drink and drive. It was his fault that Todd may never live to see his baby.

How could she be like that? How could she lay blame and not forgive him? Jesus died on the cross and paid for everyone's sins. She had to forgive the man who did this to her Todd. As she closed her eyes, she silently prayed, *God, this is the hardest thing I've ever had to do, but I pray for the strength and humility to forgive. My pride beckons me not to forgive that man for doing this to Todd, but I know my anger against him will only hurt myself. Be with Todd and protect him. In Christ's name, I pray. Amen.*

Taking heed of the nurse's advice, Charlene quietly kissed his brow and slowly arose from her seat. Steadily, the woman guided Charlene out of the stagnant room and down to the boisterous café. Halfway there, a shakiness and unsteadiness overwhelmed Charlene's entire body. It felt like a horrifying nightmare, and as she registered her mind back into reality, she screamed in terror, "No! I can't do it. I have to go back to Todd. What if he wakes up, and I'm not there? I have to be there with him."

The nurse stared at her, calm and composed as she articulated, "Ma'am, beg my pardon, but you should eat. You'll just make yourself suffer if you don't. You can quickly grab something and go back to the room if you wish."

Charlene was too tired to argue with the nurse, so she did as she was told. As she strolled back to Todd's room, with her small tray of food, she couldn't believe that any of this had happened. It was a horrendous nightmare that she hoped she would soon awake from. When Todd would wake up from this dreadful coma, everything would eventually run its normal course once again. If she could just get through the next few weeks, or even months ahead, she knew everything would be fine.

Drowsiness overtook her, with the baby coming and all as she calmly relaxed in the chair next to Todd. As she dozed off into a deep, restful sleep, a dreadful dream evolved in her mind. Although she was not actually at the crash, a reenactment of what could have happened spun through her head. She could hear Todd yelping in pain, "I love you, Char. Take care, my beautiful."

All of a sudden, she could see the doctors rush Todd away, and she helplessly cried out, "No, he's not dead! He's not."

As she tossed back and forth on the chair, she awoke startled and promptly glanced to where Todd was lying soundless. He was all right. She just needed to get that through her head. The doctors couldn't be right, they just couldn't. She wouldn't let them take her Todd away. They needed him, the baby and her.

When Todd and Charlene were first married, all he had talked about was someday having children. He loved kids more than anybody knew how. That was his ultimate dream, and finally, it was coming true. But she never told him, and now, it may be too late.

As her thoughts drifted in and out of her mind, a doctor in a white jacket and black, straight pants ambled into the peaceful room. "Eh-hem, Mrs. Carter, I don't mean to disturb you, but we must talk immediately. Something important has come up."

As Charlene stared narrowly at the doctor, she wasn't sure she wanted to listen to anything he had to say. He had might as well just leave her alone. "Can it wait? I am not much in the mood to leave my Todd, ever!" she stammered.

"It's an emergency, ma'am," the doctor replied in a steady but firm tone. Slowly, she arose and followed the doctor out of the quiet room. Whatever he had to tell her, she would sooner or later hear. Might as well get it over with.

Bad News

As she briskly followed the doctor through the crowded hallway, he finally directed her into a small room off to the left. After she brushed her short, blond hair behind her ears, she whispered a prayer under her breath, "Dear God, I pray that nothing is wrong with Todd. I know I can't raise our baby alone. Please God, protect him." She immediately slid her hand across her belly, which was barely sticking out.

"Right this way, ma'am." The doctor motioned for her to come inside a quiet, dreary office.

She swiftly blinked back the overwhelming tears as she tried to convince herself that this conversation had absolutely no relation to Todd whatsoever.

"Hello, Mrs. Carter, I am Dr. Jens. I have terrible news, and being that it is urgent, I thought you would want to know that…"

She zoned out of the present and into her deep, confusing thoughts as her mind trailed off for a brief moment. *Not really. I don't want to know my husband is not going to survive the accident. All I want is to be with him, holding his hand, and telling him that it is going to be okay.*

Interrupting her reflection on Todd, the doctor abruptly continued, "Dr. Stella, telephoned me just a short while ago, and she told me she has received your test results back."

Glaring in disbelief, she wasn't sure how to react to his statement. Well, did he know anything? Was something seriously wrong with her? He couldn't just worry her like this. Her husband had been involved in a severe car accident the night before and was traumatized in a serious state of a coma, and now, something was wrong with her. What was going on? How could God let such things happen to her and the people she loved?

"Do you know anything, Doctor? Is it life-threatening?" Charlene stared at the doctor, her mouth wide open. Everything had to be okay. It just had to be.

The doctor slowly replied as he regained his composure, "I was not informed about your condition. All I know is that Dr. Stella needs to speak to you as soon as possible."

"How soon? I mean, Todd needs me, and I can't just leave him there alone in that lonesome hospital room." She tried to be brave. She really did. But how could she make the best out of all of this? Nothing could be decidedly worse. She would just have to pray and trust that everything would turn out for the better.

"She reported that indeed it was an emergency, Mrs. Carter. The sooner you see her, the better," the professional doctor firmly stated.

As she pondered about her life for a moment, she suddenly recalled that in a few weeks it would be Christmas. If only Todd would wake up to spend the cheery holidays with her. She wiped her teary-eyed face as she managed to trail behind the doctor back through the stuffy, crammed hallways. As she neared the area, close by Todd's room, she just couldn't find the courage to descend a few floors to see Dr. Stella. Not now.

"I cannot handle any more bad news," she stammered, maintaining the pain that swirled within her. She briskly scooted inside Todd's quiet room where he solemnly lay on a bed in the corner.

Bursting into sudden tears, Charlene grasped a hold of her husband's hand and glanced down toward the floor, so nobody could see her anxiety and pain. All of a sudden, a loud, crashing thud boomed through the entire second floor like roars of cheering in a stadium. Reacting to the disturbing noise, Charlene darted out of the room to see all the chaos. A woman with shoulder-length, light-brown hair stormed out of the room next to Todd's. What had happened? Crying softly, the woman settled herself down on a wooden bench in the waiting room. Slowly, Charlene sat down beside her, and noticing a similarity to one of her old friends, she courageously asked, "Marcy, is that you?"

The woman glanced up and suddenly was aware of the stunned look on Charlene's face. "Charlene, I haven't seen you in years. At least not since high school."

"What's wrong? I heard an awful sound, and I wasn't sure what had happened."

Marcy quickly wiped her tearstained eyes. "That man in there"—she pointed shakily to the room next to Todd's—"is my husband. I was so excited when the hospital notified me that my husband, Rick, had awakened from a coma." She turned away abruptly and took a deep, long breath. Charlene urged her to continue.

"Well, about a year ago, Rick and I had decided upon doing a missions trip in Africa. We had everything sorted out—flight tickets, where we were going to live for the next three months, and which school to transfer the kids to. Rick took three months of vacation leave from work, and we just knew that God was calling us to do this. The day before we departed, Rick received an important call. He was to be on duty for the next week at the fire station due to a coworker calling in sick."

Intently, Charlene listened, eager to hear the rest of Marcy's story.

"What happened next?"

"We discussed him flying out a week later, which seemed like the only reasonable solution to our dilemma. As planned, the kids and I flew out the next day; however, during our flight to Africa,

I almost wondered if God was closing the doors from us going because of Rick's sudden call to work. Nevertheless, I kept urging myself that it was God's plan for us to go and minister. To be honest, I believe it was a sign for us not to leave, but at the time, I was unwilling to listen because I was so sure it was what God wanted us to do."

Tears rained endlessly down Marcy's sweet face as she adjusted her position on the bench.

"Rick never came…he never came. I was becoming so worried and helpless, waiting for him all hours of the night. About two months after our arrival, I wondered if this was his secret way of leaving me. But then, I received a call on May 20, the day after my accusation; it was the hospital. They had phoned to notify me that Rick had been involved in a serious fire accident the night after our departure to Africa and had been injured very seriously. They had tried to call sooner, but they couldn't get a hold of me. Charlene, I heard about my husband's accident two months after it happened."

"Do you mind if I ask how it happened?"

"Well, at about six o'clock that day, a frayed wire in an old house suddenly sparked, and it was only a matter of time before the building was up in flames. Upon their arrival, Rick and two other firefighters—Nathaniel and Josh—had immediately undertaken their mission to rescue four children who were trapped inside. Meanwhile, the rest of the team worked to silence the crackling, hot fire that darkened the atmosphere around them."

Charlene shared her friend's anguish as they both cried, releasing the sorrow that gripped their souls from within. Marcy's voice twirled into a shaky tone as she continued the tragic story.

"Everyone got out safe except for Rick. When Nathaniel realized Rick was still inside the raging, fiery building, he and Josh quickly reentered in search of him. When they did finally find him, Josh explained to me that a board had fallen on Rick's head and had knocked him out cold. I am surprised he is still alive."

The tears were streaming down Charlene's soft face as she held another mysterious secret deep inside her. The pain erupted once again as if she had lost a loved one.

"While balancing Rick in their arms, Josh and Nathaniel tried to escape the hot flames that burdened them; however, in their attempt, Nathaniel somehow got trapped. From how Josh described it, he said that Nathaniel was right behind him. When he glanced back, Nathaniel was lying on the floor behind burning, fallen boards, continuously yelling, "I love you. Take care, my beautiful." He said the first part he heard was a bit muffled, but the last part was as clear as a bell. He tried to free Nathaniel from the inevitable prison of death, but he couldn't do it alone. Nathaniel urged Josh to leave him there and save Rick's and his life in return. He gave up his life, so Rick and Josh could live."

The pieces slowly began fitting in the mysterious puzzle as Charlene continued to listen. Was it true?

"Meanwhile, I was still in Africa. When I received the urgent yet devastating call, I tried to book a flight out. I did not realize that I was not allowed to leave the country."

"Why? What do you mean? Are you saying that today was the first day you've seen Rick?" Charlene was so confused.

"Yes, today is the very first day I have been on good, solid, Canadian ground in ten months. You see, when I went to book a flight, the airports had just closed down. Nobody was to depart from or enter Africa. You don't know how hard it is to wait, knowing your husband is dying, and you can't do anything about it. There was a runaway convict who had escaped from one of the jails. The police finally found him about a week ago. I was scared spitless while this was all happening, worrying about Rick and then the man who was wanted for treason. I trusted God with all of my heart to bring us through. And he did." She paused a short moment as she wiped away a runaway tear.

"I was so thrilled to see Rick today. He woke up from a coma about two months ago. He had to learn to walk and talk all over again as if he was a child. This isn't the worst part of it all, Charlene. He doesn't remember me. I thought he had to remember me. He forced me to leave and never to return. I just wanted to hear his deep, comforting voice. You know, it's been so long since I heard that man talk. He threw a flower vase on the floor just a few feet in front of me. I am so scared; I just don't know what to do."

Charlene couldn't even imagine or bear the thought of Todd not remembering her. How could the man you love just forget about you? If only she could comfort her friend during this tragic time.

"Marcy, would you like to go for lunch? I am getting a little bit hungry. Todd should be fine—"

Marcy instantly interrupted her, "What's wrong with Todd? I am so sorry. I was blabbering on about Rick, and I never asked you why you were here." Charlene suddenly began crying uncontrollably. She didn't know if she could ever find the strength to share the tragedy. Well, if Marcy had the courage to disclose her devastating story, then she could too.

Slowly, the two ladies sauntered downstairs to the café where dark-green booths outlined the brown painted room. A few ordinary tables occupied the middle of the room where numerous people were eating joyously. How could anyone feel so blissful when they were in a hospital where their loved ones lay helpless?

After ordering their food, the two ladies sat down at a small, green booth in the corner. The noise in the café was irritating, but Charlene tried to drown out the chatter of people talking as she revealed the terrible tragedy to her friend.

"It's been really hard these past couple of months," Charlene began. She paused a brief moment as she held the agonizing tears back. "Todd was recently in an awful accident. As a matter of fact, it was just last night that a drunk driver swerved and crashed into Todd's vehicle."

Marcy reached across the table and tenderly squeezed Charlene's cold, dry hands. "Is Todd all right?" Marcy asked, feeling her friend's excruciating distress.

During the next hour, Charlene jabbered on about how the doctors explained to her that Todd's chance of waking up from a coma was not very likely. She openly shared her deepest, darkest secrets with Marcy.

"Todd lost his job three weeks ago. It's been really hard on him."

"I am so sorry to hear that. What happened? I don't mean to be prying, but how did Todd lose his job?" Marcy curiously asked.

As the tears trickled down her cheek like a waterfall spilling into its waters, Charlene sniffled as she softly whispered, "I don't know. He barely talks to me anymore. Sometimes, I wonder if I made a mistake in marrying him. It's not like I didn't know him well enough before we were married. We have known each other since kindergarten from Sunday school class."

"Do you still have that regret?"

"No, I don't. I love that man more than life itself. I just wish I could have been there for him, the way he was for me." It brought back memories when Todd had continuously comforted her while she was mourning over her loss of Nate. The pain deepened greatly as she shared how Todd would ignore everything she had tried to tell him. That was why she had never been open with him about the baby. Expecting it to be a time of joy, she waited until he overcame this strange outburst.

Lately, he would either yell at her or ignore her for no specific reason. She loved him very much and tried to give him the space he needed to overcome this hard trial in his life. Did he think she would look at him any differently because he could not provide for his family at the time being? For the past couple of weeks, he had been so irritated by something, but she could not figure out what was troubling him.

As the ladies eventually turned the conversation to their childhood memories together, Charlene and Marcy both forgot all their worries.

What's Wrong With Me?

As the sun slowly seeped through the blinds that draped over the sizeable window, Charlene awoke startled by the strident commotion occurring in the hospital. Straightening herself, she slid her hands through her short, blond hair to fix any stray pieces.

After completing her quick hairdo, she instantaneously glanced over to see if Todd was still all right. His face was becoming paler than ever before, and his hands seemed unusually cold. Slowly, she grabbed his firm hand and gripped it tightly, fearing that the doctors were right, he may never wake up. As the frightful thought pierced her insides, Dr. Jens swiftly sauntered into the room.

Quietly, he whispered, "We did a few tests on him yesterday, and the chance of him surviving his severe head injury is about 20 percent." She stared at him as if the world was coming to an end.

"Does that mean that the likelihood of him waking up is never? No! No! You must have made a mistake. You're wrong. He will wake up. I know he will. I just know it!" Charlene screamed as the agony tore at her.

"Keep it down, ma'am. This is a hospital, and there are other patients resting," a nurse calmly stated.

Crying with all her heart's desire, the nurse slowly guided her out of the room and nicely asked her to exit the hospital until she could contain herself.

"No, I cannot leave my Todd. They say he is going to die, and I will not let them take him away from me. Never! He needs me," Charlene cried out in pain.

The nurse immediately assisted her downstairs and politely requested she leave the premises for a few days. As Charlene panted for Todd, they forced her to leave and mourn at home where she would be of no burden to anyone. The hospital was similar to a library. They both required people to be calm and quiet; therefore, she finally gave in, afraid they may never let her enter the building again if she refused to oblige.

Sluggishly, she tottered toward her black Durango, and climbed inside. Whispering a prayer, she solemnly said, "God, you know how much I love Todd. He means the world to me. I don't look at him any differently now that he has lost his job. I love him the same, and even more. Don't let him die; he's barely had a life to live. In Jesus' name, I pray. Amen."

The ride home was slow but manageable. It seemed as if the universe was coming to a sudden end. Right now, she wished it would, except for the fact that her son or daughter would never live to see the world nor would have the opportunity to have a special relationship with Jesus, the way she did.

She was a strong Christian; she really was. She had accepted Christ as her personal Savior when she was four years old. She just was reaching a bumpy patch in her walk with the Lord that made her doubt if he was really there for her. "God is our refuge and strength, a very present help in trouble" (Psalms 46:1, NASB). It didn't seem as though God was lifting a burden off her to help carry the load. For some reason, it seemed as if he was placing all the junk in her life. It felt as though someone had a great life in the world, and God had just thrown all the bad in hers. Why would God do such a thing?

At the time, she would not understand his wonderful plan for her life. She just couldn't comprehend why Nate had died, and now, Todd was slipping away too. Why had God let all this happen? Did he have a reason? Well, if he did, it didn't seem like a very good one to her. It's not as though she didn't pray and believe in God because she did. She just wondered where her walk with him was.

Striding up the long walkway, she screeched the creaky door open to their rustic, old home. As she glanced around the neat and tidy living room, she noticed there was a voicemail. Unhurriedly, she pressed the answering machine button, and to her astonishment, a strange woman's voice overflowed in the quiet room.

"Hi, Charlene, this is Dr. Stella, your doctor. I was informed that you received my message from Dr. Jens this morning. I have been given your test results back, and it is very important that I speak to you immediately. Hopefully, I will be seeing you shortly. Thank you. Bye now."

How could she fail to remember that Dr. Jens had instructed her to pay a visit to the doctor's office early that morning? Oh, wait, she was pregnant, her husband was dying, and now, she had this to add to the entire trauma. Everything in her right mind was occurring amiss. Did every family live like this, always wondering what next strange event would result in the mystery of life?

Remembering the hospital's strict orders, she recollected that she was forbidden to enter inside the tranquil building. She was highly restricted for a minimal of two days. Well, it was not going to take her just two days to battle this sudden tragedy; it could take her forever to adjust to the fact that Nate had died, and now, Todd was dying too. Maybe if she promised wholeheartedly not to make such a scene again, they would allow her to be of company to her husband.

Quickly, she jumped inside her black Durango and zoomed off. When she arrived, she slowly directed her vehicle into a free parking slot and marched back inside the hospital.

"Mrs. Carter, I believe we kindly asked you to take some time to rest at your own home. We know this has been really hard for you, and we would prefer you not to enter the building until you have maintained your uncontrollable temper," the same feisty nurse advised her.

"Yes, I clearly remember, but I forgot I had an appointment with Dr. Stella. I promise that I will not bother anyone." Charlene struggled to be persuasive.

"Well, you obviously are not doing a fine job of that. You are already bothering me. And about your doctor's appointment, you should have remembered you had arrangements before performing a rude scene in the hospital earlier. I am very sorry, but you are not permitted to come here until a few days have passed. Please respect the policy of our hospital. As persistent as you try to be to convince me, don't think for one second you can fool me," the nurse snapped. She was becoming very impatient and irritant with Charlene's determined effort.

As the nurse finished her harsh statement, Dr. Stella wandered over after her lunch break to settle the aggravating argument between the two. As Dr. Stella approached, she quickly ended the dispute, "Tonya, it's an emergency that I speak to Charlene." Glaring at Charlene as if it was her fault, the nurse backed off slowly as if she thought that she should be in charge of what Charlene could and couldn't do in the hospital. However, before Tonya had the chance of starting yet another quarrel, Dr. Stella directly ushered Charlene to her office.

If it was an emergency, something had to be wrong, right? Maybe it was good news, and Dr. Stella could not wait to notify her. Oh no! Could something be wrong with the baby? She prayed with her whole heart that if something were wrong, it would have to do with her and would have no relation to the precious life she held inside her. As the thoughts crawled in and out of her mind, Dr. Stella explained what was wrong.

"Charlene, I have good news and bad news. Which would you like to hear first?"

"The good news would be better right now," Charlene briskly answered, afraid of what the unpleasant information might be.

"The good news is that the baby is completely fine. He or she is very healthy." She paused a brief moment as her voice reverted into a serious tone. "The critical news, however, is that you are now a victim of cancer."

Absorbing the words, Charlene thought carefully. Maybe she had not heard right. Was she really sick?

"Charlene, you have a serious case of cancer. Your examination has proved that you have a brain tumor."

"I don't understand. I am perfectly fine. You must have the wrong person because I feel as I usually do, quite normal."

"Calm down. There is a slight chance that you will live. We are not completely sure how big your tumor is. That is why I am sending you for a CT scan in Calgary. Your scheduled appointment is in three days because, fortunately, someone canceled out. I will be seeing you shortly."

"But I have a husband who is nearly dying and a baby on the way. I certainly cannot have a brain tumor. Are you sure this is necessary?"

"The sooner we catch it, the better chance you have of survival."

With that, Dr. Stella swiftly stepped out of the room to deal with the rest of her patients. Why was God taking her through this? Why would he do this to her? It felt as though he didn't care about her at all. She could not handle any more disastrous events. She just couldn't.

Praying as she left the hospital, she asked God for the strength to uphold her during this time of trial. There was one thing she knew: God would walk beside her and guide her through this journey she had never expected to travel on. Life was definitely full of surprises.

A Time of Prayer

Slowly, the sun arose across the brisk, blue sky as the wind steadied itself over the rich, green grass. When Charlene awoke the next morning, she could barely think. The former day was too much to even grasp. It was a horrifying nightmare she could never awake from. She just had to deal with the circumstance because there was no way of escaping or hiding from it. She had to face up to the fact that she now had cancer. There was nothing she could do about it. She just wondered how everything could change from a dazzling fairy tale to a dreadful nightmare in one year.

Yearning to share her feelings with somebody, she only wished her family was there to comfort her during this doubting time. Her parents lived all the way in South Carolina, thousands of miles away; therefore, she did not intend to overwhelm them with this dramatic tragedy, especially after her father's heart attack a month ago.

Staring widely, Charlene debated between calling her older sister, Sandra, or not. Finally, she decided against it because Sandra was just so busy with her own family; there was no need to burden her with Charlene's hectic life as well.

All of a sudden, an amazing idea thundered through her mind. She *did* have someone to talk to. In fact, it was her very best friend. Her Heavenly Father would be the perfect one to unveil her deepest thoughts to. He would always listen to her needs and comfort her during this dark valley in her life. This was too much for her to carry alone. God would be there with her, holding her up when she was about to fall. Even though she doubted him sometimes, she still was eager to talk to him. It didn't always feel like he listened or was always there, but he always was; she just didn't know it. He cared about her; he truly did. All in good time she would realize it.

Steadily kneeling down, she folded her tiny hands and prayed, unlocking the door to her heart. "Dear Heavenly Father, I come before you now, brokenhearted and in deep continuous sorrow. I cannot comprehend the whole plan you have in store for me, but I am very afraid that Todd may die. He's everything to me, and I do not know what I would do without him. The pain and agony deepen inside me during this dark and dreary time, but I pray that the best will evolve from all of this. God, I don't understand why I have a brain tumor and why I am going to have a baby at a time like this, but I place these things in your hands."

Endlessly, she poured her heart out to God. She did not always understand everything, but she did know that God had the picture all painted out. He knew the outcome of this journey; it was comforting to know that he did. Was it to get her attention? "I am here for you, Charlene. I have a special plan for you so don't lose hope. This will not be an easy path to travel on, but I promise you that I will walk beside you all the way."

Trusting God with her whole heart, she dressed herself and wiped the dried tears from her stained eyes. Calmly, she staggered out of her bedroom and into the kitchen to prepare breakfast. Pouring some cheerios into a glass bowl, she gladly filled her empty stomach and positioned herself on a comfy, pink cushion that covered an alder stool. A peace renewed her weary soul, and she felt at rest with God. He was everything to her; he truly was. He would help her through. He always did.

The day slowly announced its ending as the sun slowly set across the horizon, and the stars glittered in their scattered pattern across the royal-blue sky. Dimly, the moon lay peacefully in the dark night atmosphere.

After Charlene quickly said a prayer, she crawled inside her cozy, welcoming bed. Stretching her feet under the warm blanket, she murmured under her breath as she dozed into a deep, restful sleep, "Good night, Todd. I love you, sweetheart. I will see you tomorrow, my love."

The next morning arrived promptly as if she never got a wink of sleep at all. She was determined to spend the final day with Todd before she had to drive to Calgary no matter what Tonya said. The thought of being with him sent jitters through her body as if it were the first date all over again. She only wished that it was. He used to take her for long romantic walks around a beautiful park near their house when they first were married. The lovely strolls were usually accompanied by scenic evenings as the bright sun set into a majestic orange across the painted sky. It was like a glimpse of heaven before their eyes.

Without delay, she quickly prepared herself for the day ahead and speedily raced to her Durango parked outside. It was a gorgeous day, the sun gleaming across the perfectly blue sky as it reflected off the icy snow that sheeted the thick ground. As she drove to the hospital in silence, she noticed a pile of unpaid bills lying on the dashboard. Decidedly, she made a quick detour to the bank to pay off what she owed.

Gradually, she parked her car into a parallel spot behind a red Mustang convertible. Her Durango looked incomparably large beside it.

Sauntering inside the loud, noisy bank, she tottered toward a slot where a little, old lady cheerfully greeted her.

"How can I help you, ma'am?" the petite, short woman asked.

"I was wondering if I could pay off these bills?" Charlene answered, handing her the stack.

"Oh, of course. Let me see here." She hesitated for a second as she rang Charlene's bankbook through the scanner. "Ma'am, I believe there is a problem with your account." Her facial expression revealed a sense of worry.

"What could be the matter? We had plenty of money in our account the last time I was here, which was only a few weeks ago."

"Well, your account is completely dried out. It is bankrupt."

How in the world could so much money be used in such a short period of time? The last time she was there was two weeks prior to the day. There was no possible way that such an amount could disappear just like that. Or could it?

"I don't understand. Are you absolutely sure that we have no money in our account? It must be a mistake. Maybe you should check it again," Charlene calmly declared.

Suddenly, the woman's mannerisms reflected a prejudice air in her encounter with Charlene, and she embarrassed her in front of everyone. "No mistake here. Like I said before, there is no cash in your account. Zero. Would you like me to spell that out for you?" The snippety lady's voice was spinning furiously at Charlene.

The confusion of the circumstance was unimaginable. How was she going to live without any money? This was the worst thing that could top off the whole trauma. Appalling incidents just kept adding to the complicated puzzle of Charlene's hectic life. What was God taking her through and why?

Embarrassed by the entire situation, she immediately fled to the safety of her vehicle. No strange eyes could stare at her or think she was totally wacko. In a brisk maneuver, she quickly shoved the keys into the ignition and zoomed off into the direction of the hospital.

Thankfully, Tonya was nowhere in sight; therefore, Charlene had no problem sneaking up to visit Todd. However, as she neared the doorway to his room, she suddenly recognized the same crisp, feisty voice. It was Tonya's familiar face inside Rick's room next door. Hesitantly, Charlene ducked inside Todd's room before Tonya had the chance of noticing her. She did not need a repeat of the day before yesterday's episode.

As she sat down on the bed beside Todd, she softly whispered, "God, hear my prayer. Protect this man that I dearly love. I cannot imagine what I would do without him. I didn't know what I would do without Nathaniel after he passed away, but you brought along Todd all in good time. Just continue to be with him. I know I cannot bear to lose him too."

It was almost as if Todd had heard her praying. As she tightly gripped his sturdy hand, she felt it slightly move beneath her palm. There was hope. They just needed a miracle.

The Letter

Awaking the next morning, Charlene opened her stiff, crusty eyes. She glanced at the room around her, noticing she was still at the hospital.

What am I doing here? I must have fallen asleep here last night.

Quickly, she gathered her things off the clean, tidy floor and abruptly stood to her feet. Dizziness and nausea overpowered her, and she instantly sat down again. She rubbed her sweaty forehead and itched her sore eyes.

What's wrong with me? Why do I feel so awful?

Instantly, the apparent reason she was sick stormed through her mind as she gazed at her round stomach that was barely bulging. It was the baby growing inside her that created a nauseous feeling. Every woman faced pregnancy sickness. Why had she overlooked herself?

After the queasiness and wooziness passed, she arose and stepped closer to Todd's bed. She tenderly kissed his forehead and delicately whispered in his ear, "Don't you worry about me, Todd. Everything will be fine. I will be back tonight. I love you, darling."

She quickly exited the hospital before the tears had a chance to escape from her eyelids. It was hard to leave Todd that way, alone and helpless. But there was nothing she could do.

Swiftly, she scrambled inside her Durango and switched the heat on, allowing the warmth to wash away her worries. God would have to help her through the day ahead because alone she faced it weak and afraid of what the end result would be.

The drive seemed to drag on forever as she carefully maneuvered her vehicle through the chaotic traffic. Finally, she arrived at the Calgary hospital. As she slipped inside, an overpowering nervousness shot through her veins, and she rapidly took a seat in the waiting room before she passed out from worry. Bowing her head, she silently prayed, not caring how people would react to her unvoiced conversation with God. At this moment, all she wanted was to share her heart with him; he was the only one who would understand.

God, I am very frightened. Help me to accept the fact that I have a brain tumor and give me your strength to deal with whatever you bring my way. Whatever happens, I will always serve you. Amen.

As she lifted her head, a nauseas sensation shot through her entire body. She squeezed her eyelids shut as if it relieved some of the tension. Battling the pain that erupted inside her, she clutched the sides of the chair for support. It was the same achiness that had overwhelmed her earlier that morning. She breathed deeply, until finally the terrible feeling subsided. Several minutes later a heavier woman called her name and directed her into a quiet room. The test was done without delay, and Charlene patiently waited until a broad, tall man with a dark-blond comb over ambled into the silent room.

"I'm Dr. Smith. I believe your doctor, Dr. Stella, was right. You do have a brain tumor, and it is cancerous. The good thing is it is very small. Surgically, it can be removed with very little problem. However, there is the risk that you may not survive the surgery as in all surgeries of course."

Her heart felt like it had stopped pounding as Dr. Smith's words crashed over her like a strong wave. It *was* a brain tumor.

She didn't always understand God's purpose, but God had a reason for this, and she trusted him that everything would work out.

As she departed from the busy city, the sky was beginning to fade into a rich amber as the sun slowly depressed from the sky. Darkness began to shadow across the road until a royal-blue hung in the atmosphere and the moon seeped through the painted sky. The dimness overwhelmed her as she tried to maintain her vehicle on the road. She was beginning to feel drowsy and overtired but urged herself to continue the long drive home. Thankfully, she arrived in Edmonton safely, and she instantaneously redirected her black Durango in the direction of the hospital. Her heart longed to see Todd.

When she got there, she briskly scampered up two flights of stairs until she reached Todd's room. He looked so sad and weary, lying there so helpless in the corner. As she sat down in her usual chair next to him, she decisively pulled out a piece of scrap paper from her purse and scribbled a quick letter to her parents. She felt bad burdening them with this heavy load, but she had no one else to turn to for guidance. She was coming to the end of her ropes; she didn't know what else she could do.

First, she had absolutely no money; second, she had a cancerous brain tumor; third, her husband had been in a serious accident; and fourth, she was expecting a baby all at the same time. She had no other choice but to disclose her hectic life to someone. She knew for one thing that she could not battle this on her own. Slowly, the words erupted in her mind as she hastily wrote them on a blank, white piece of paper.

Dear Mom and Dad,

I did not intend for this letter to be all about my troublesome life by any means, and I even second-guessed myself about sending this to you. However, the past couple of weeks, I have been traveling a *life journey, and I am in desperate need of your parental guidance. It began a few weeks ago when Todd lost his job and has only gotten worse. I don't always understand what God has in store for us, and it just seems as though my life is full of endless conflicts, one after another. A few nights ago, Todd was involved in a serious accident. I wanted to tell you right away, but I did not desire to burden you with my wearisome life. Managing as best as I can, I have come to realize that this is what seems to be an unending journey, and I need your prayers during this doubting period in my life. Sometimes, I feel as though God doesn't care about me anymore. I know it is wrong to think those thoughts because they are not true. "The Lord Himself goes before you and will be with you; He will never leave you nor forsake you. Do not be afraid; do not be discouraged" (Deuteronomy 31:8, niv). I am scared and dismayed. Everything in my life seems to be getting worse. Just yesterday, I found out that all our money in our account has disappeared. Amidst this, I am still recovering from the loss of Nate, and now, I am faced with losing Todd too. Please keep Todd and me in your prayers during this time. As you can see, my life never stops, and I hardly have a chance to breathe. I hate dropping this burdensome load upon you both and would love to lighten it by sharing some wonderful news. I am pregnant and am expecting in eight months. I cannot believe I am finally going to be a mother. Thank you for always being there for me. I love you both very much and will keep you posted. Talk to you soon.*

All my prayers and love,
Charlene

Unquestionably, she left out the part about her brain tumor and Todd being in a coma. There was no need to shower her parents with her disconcerting life. All she needed right now was someone to share her affliction with, to guide her. She felt horrible bothering her parents with all the trauma taking place in her life, but it was the only people she could turn to.

Barely keeping her eyes open, she rested her head on the rough chair and dozed off into a comforting sleep. It had been a long, hard day, and the rest would do her a whole lot of good. She would have to deal with the money situation later. Perhaps for the time being she could find a suitable job. Either way, she had to pay monthly finances on their home, not to mention Todd's medical expenses.

Life was definitely not slowing down any time soon. She would just have to hang in there and pray that God would carry her through it all. At least she knew that God was her one best friend that she could always count on, in the good times and the bad. He was truly more than a friend. He was also her Heavenly Father.

Surprising Visit

Gradually, the days slowly passed. Christmas was approaching, and Charlene had nothing to show for the special occasion. It had been a difficult month with all the chaotic stress, and she decided not to decorate her house or make a big deal of the holiday. No festive turkey dinner or Christmas music would accompany the joyful season this year. She would pretend as if it were any other normal day in her life. The only event of the season that she would celebrate was Jesus' birthday, nothing more. It was the happiest time of year, but she was definitely not in the mood to be joyful. Not without her precious Todd.

Last year had been her final Christmas with Nate, which had never been expected. This year was supposed to be her first Christmas with Todd, and he wasn't even there to celebrate it with her. Her life was a never-ending, bumpy rollercoaster. It never slowed down for her to jump off. It just kept speeding up.

As Christmas announced it's coming, the snow gracefully fell, shimmering delicately across the rooftops. Day after day, it gradually formed into a fluffy, white blanket as it covered the city edge to edge. As the Christmas lights glistened over the edge of roofs, the snow glittered down as the glow of the lights shone through.

Christmas Eve arrived without any hurry and diminished just as slowly as it came. Tomorrow would be even worse. The thought of spending Christmas without Todd stung Charlene to the very core, and she immediately pushed the unwelcoming idea away. Maybe she could spend it with Todd. Being at the hospital on Christmas didn't sound too inviting, but it would be more pleasurable than staying at home alone.

Finally, it was Christmas morning, and as the sun slowly crawled out of its warm, cozy bed, it shone across the light-blue sky. Slipping from beneath her covers, Charlene hastily arose when she heard the continuous ring of a doorbell. Frantically, she raced to the antique front door. As she creaked it open, her facial expression reflected her surprise.

"Mom and Dad, what are you doing here?"

"Darling, we received your letter and thought it would be appropriate to come and visit you. You should have told us sooner," her mother sweetly uttered, embracing her daughter. She was a sweet, old lady with a tender and loving heart, yet she also had a precise way about her. Her body shape was slim and short, and her hair was mostly blond with streaks of gray outlining the roots.

Inviting them inside the warmth of her house, Charlene instantly set the coffee on to brew. After it was prepared, she poured it into mugs as they sat down around the kitchen table.

"We are so happy for you and Todd, Charlene. You are expecting that wee little bundle of joy that will brighten your world," her father began as he scratched his scruffy, gray beard. He was a tall, slender man with hazel-brown eyes, and his thick, short hair was as white as snow.

"It should hold the fort down for a while," he finished as he graciously handed her a gift. *What was that supposed to mean?* Unwrapping it slowly, she found a cute, little outfit that could be worn for either a boy or a girl. A bit embarrassed by what she did, she thought, *Why didn't I open the card first? Oh well, it's too late.* As she tore open the envelope, she uncovered a beautiful card with a manger scene decorating the front and on the top it said, Merry Christmas. Peering inside, she read the fine print belonging to her mother.

> *Charlene,*
>
> *We hope your Christmas is filled with many blessings. Keep trusting in God, and he will show you the way. We will always be here for you if you ever need us. Have a wonderful Christmas.*
>
> *Love and prayers,*
> *Mom and Dad*

It was sweet but short. Her mother definitely had a special, unique way of writing cards.

"Did you find the enclosed money, Charlene?" her mother kindly asked.

Suddenly, Charlene realized there was a cheque of fifteen thousand dollars stuck inside the envelope. She could not accept this expensive gift. However, there was no need to argue with her parents; they had made up their minds. Thanking them for their generosity, she excused herself to get ready for the day. After combing her short, ruffled, blond hair and getting herself dressed, the three of them hopped inside Charlene's Durango and drove to the hospital to visit Todd.

"Now, where is my son-in-law? My daughter could not have found anyone more suitable than him. He is perfect for her," her mother cheerfully announced as they briskly scampered up to his hospital room. Although her parents had never been very fond of Nate, Charlene had loved him with her whole heart. God had intended for them to be together even though it was just for a short time.

As they entered the silent room, Dr. Jens, Tonya, and three other nurses were huddling over Todd's side. What was going on?

"Excuse me, I am going to have to ask you all to leave right now. We are having some difficulties," Tonya politely instructed.

"Your husband has stopped breathing, and we are doing everything we can," another nurse kindly explained.

Praying that she had not heard right, Charlene was completely devastated. "My Todd? My husband? Is he going to be all right?"

Tonya, a little bit annoyed, glared at her and snapped, "We are doing everything we can. He is still alive, but he is having a hard time breathing. Please take a seat and wait outside. Thank you." With that, petite and feisty Tonya retreated to help Dr. Jens and the others.

Her parents obeyed the strict command and assisted Charlene to the waiting room. Christmas was supposed to be a joyous time. Why did this have to happen? The pain and agony tore at her insides as it developed into flaming tears. How could God let Todd die? Courageously, she locked away the tenseness deep inside her before it escaped into shrieking words. She didn't need to get kicked out of the hospital again.

After twenty minutes, her dad broke the complete silence that stung the air. "Charlene, do you mind if we pray with you? This is going to be a testing time, but if you trust in God, he will bring you through."

Her parents obviously had no idea to all that was going on because Charlene hadn't told them. She had not yet revealed the secret of her brain tumor. Slowly, she answered, "I would really like that, Dad." Spilling from the corners of her eyes, the tears overflowed down her face as her mother put her arm around her frightened daughter.

"What's wrong, Charlene?" her mother curiously asked when she noticed Charlene crying.

Charlene couldn't hold it inside her any more. She swallowed the anxiety that was burning up her throat as she replied, "I have been diagnosed with a cancerous brain tumor. I am going to have to have surgery."

"Darling, we did not know," her mother gently said as the tears softly streamed down her angelic face. Her voice reflected how scared she was for Charlene.

Her father tried to sound brave as he began to pray, "God, comfort Charlene with your undivided love as she faces the many challenges that lay ahead. I pray that her surgery will be successful and that she would be able to continue the wonderful path of life. Be with our son-in-law, Todd. I pray that you will guide Dr. Jens in whatever he needs to do. Please also protect the little one inside Charlene. We lay all these things in your hands, for you are the Most High. Amen."

After a long, dragging hour, Dr. Jens strolled out of Todd's room. Charlene prayed wholeheartedly as he sauntered toward her. God would take care of her, and she just had to leave it up to him. All she could do right now was pray that God would bring Todd through. In the meantime, she held onto everything she had left of her precious husband, Todd.

Is He?

Waiting was the hardest thing Charlene had to do, not knowing if Todd would survive or not. As Dr. Jens strode toward her, she wasn't sure how to interpret his facial expression. Did he have bad or good news? Unhurriedly, he froze in front of the trio and calmly stated, "He is breathing completely fine for now. Nevertheless, that will not eliminate the chance of him waking up. He could be in a coma for who knows how long. I can't promise you that he will come through, but keep praying, Charlene, because God does answer our prayers. He answered mine today. I thought for sure that this was the end of your husband's life. I was wrong, and who knows, I might be wrong again." He winked at her as if to let her in on his little secret—the secret that his prediction of Todd not waking up could possibly be incorrect.

Slowly, he walked away as a smile softly shone on his face. Praise the Lord! Alleluia! At least Todd was still alive. That was all Charlene cared about right now. Todd being in a coma was one thing, but him not overcoming it was another. At the moment, Todd still being in a coma didn't trouble her as long as he was all right. Maybe Christmas was a time for miracles after all.

As the days quickly passed by, life was beginning to run its normal course once again, except for the fact that Todd was not there to share the tiresome days with her. In the middle of

January, her parents left, and she felt she could at least manage on her own for a while. She was so grateful to her parents for making sure she was okay and for all their help. They truly were the best parents ever. They didn't just watch her struggle through it, but they directed and guided her along the way. Wasn't that what parents were for, to always be there?

After she saw them off and their silver Ford Edge dispersed into the cloudy, muddled fog, she slowly trudged back inside the dark, lonely house and instantly recognized the unremitting ring of a telephone. Grabbing the receiver, she timidly said, "Hello, this is Charlene speaking."

"Hi, Charlene. This is Dr. Stella. I am phoning to ask you if you have chosen to have the surgery."

Responding slowly as the jitters raced through her body, she finally answered with a shy yes. She was most grateful that her doctor was so concerned about her.

"All right, I am going to book your surgery at the end of the month. Your tumor is a priority, so I should have no trouble making you an appointment. There is a more educated surgeon in Calgary, and I would highly recommend that he perform your surgery. His name is Dr. Simon Smith. He was the doctor who spoke with you after your CT scan."

After everything was sorted out, Charlene quietly uttered, "Thank you, Dr. Stella. My appointment is on January 28 in Calgary. Is that right?

"Yes. Now you take care of yourself, Charlene. Remember that you are continuously in my prayers. Bye now."

Charlene felt a sense of hope and renewal. God would be there with her to get her through this. She just knew it.

Noticing a stack of Christmas cards on the table, she realized there was one still unopened. As she peeked inside the handmade card, she slowly soaked in the comforting words.

Dear Charlene,

We hope you have a wonderful Christmas. You have been such an incredible daughter-in-law, and although Nate is no longer here with us, you will always be welcomed in our home. A glowing smile lit Nate's face after he met you, a smile that men only have when they are deeply, truly in love, and God knew you were meant for each other. We hope to visit you sometime soon. Merry Christmas!

Love you lots,
Mom and Dad

P.S. We are so happy you have married Todd. He sounds like a fantastic man. Sorry to have missed your wedding. We were truly looking forward to it. Nate would be proud to know you are happy again and that such a fine man is looking after you. God bless.

Nate's parents had always been so good to her. As she wobbled over to the couch, tiredness suddenly swept through her like the wind rustling the leaves. Lying on the comfortable, leather chesterfield, she fell into a deep, solemn sleep. It was probably good, since having a baby and all, required more rest.

Sleeping for over three hours, Charlene instantly awoke to the sudden, thunderous sound of a dish crashing to the floor. Who was there? Shivering continuously from fright, she only wished that Todd were there to protect her. Slowly, she jerked herself upward and carefully inspected the living room. It didn't look as though someone were there. Scrambling quickly to the kitchen, Charlene stared at the floor where tiny pieces of glass were shattered across their beautiful maple hardwood.

Bracing herself, she spoke loudly, the tenseness reflecting in her voice, "Is anybody there?" When a small voice answered,

Charlene shrieked. How did anybody sneak into her house? She was almost positive she had locked the door behind her.

As the voice traveled closer, the words gradually grew crisp enough to hear. "Hello, Charlene. Is that you calling?" the mysterious person replied. Skimming the room for the strange voice, Charlene's eyes popped wide open as a mystifying person meandered toward her. Was she going crazy?

"Charlene, don't you recognize me?"

Shaking her head as if it were an awful nightmare, Charlene's rosy-red face transformed paler than snow.

The tiny woman looked at Charlene in disbelief.

"Sis, it is me, Sandra. Mother called me a few nights ago while she was here and told me what had happened. I was so worried about you. Matt took a few days off work to be with Nick, Tommy, and Alyssa. I wanted so badly to be here for you; you have always been there for me," Sandra softly responded.

Was Charlene going completely brain dead? How could she not have recognized her older sister?

For the next several minutes, Charlene updated her sister on all the details from when Todd had first been in the accident to when she had found out she had a brain tumor.

"Is he going to be all right?" Sandra asked with concern. According to Dr. Jens, he barely had a chance of surviving the crucial accident, but to Charlene, God would bring him through in his timing.

Shrugging her shoulders, Charlene tried to hold the stinging tears deep inside her. Slowly, she bent her head downward to ease the pain that thundered through her. By the edge in Charlene's voice, Sandra could tell her sister was greatly overwhelmed. Embracing one another, the two sisters stood in silence for a long, solemn moment.

Finally, Sandra quickly changed the subject and broke the stale solitude. Calmly, she stated, "I am sorry for frightening you. I let myself in with the spare key you had given me when Nate and you were first married. I was about to prepare dinner when I accidentally dropped a plate. I just quickly went to retrieve this broom." She shook the broom that was firmly gripped in her hands. That was what had happened. Nothing so minor as a dish shattering could bother Charlene after all the waves that had thunderously crashed into her life. There was one thing she knew, the high tides in life made her trust the one who was steering the boat—her Savior Jesus Christ.

After the two had supper, they decided to depart for the hospital to pay a visit to Todd. As much as she tried, Sandra could not imagine or even comprehend how hard it would be to have such a tragedy happen to Matt and her. Having three children, two boys and a little girl, was all she could handle.

For a brief moment, she paused and finally asked her sister, Charlene, if she could pray with her. A smile instantly evolved upon Charlene's sweet face. She always looked up to her sister and was relieved to have someone to share her troubles with. Grasping a hold of Todd's hand and then Sandra's, Charlene felt a tremendous weight lifted off her as the petite, older woman calmly prayed, "God, be with Charlene during this tragic time in her life. Comfort her when she needs comfort and strengthen her when she needs strength. There has been so much going on in her life, and I pray that you will walk with her the whole way. You are so merciful. Please show your unfailing mercy toward her. In Christ's name, I pray. Amen."

God's presence filled Charlene's heart. He would bring her through. She believed and trusted that he would.

Surgery

Sadly, Charlene's beloved sister, Sandra, returned home to her family within a few days. Her husband, Matt, had been called into work, forcing Sandra to shorten her stay. Life dragged on slowly not yet to its fullest. Charlene's surgery was in a few days, and she was so scared. What if Dr. Smith made a mistake? What if she didn't survive? As much as she worried, it never helped, and she just had to trust that God's plan was first. No matter how she wished she would benefit from the situation, she couldn't change his wonderful plan for her life.

Fortunately, Sandra lived in Calgary and would be assisting her to the hospital. Charlene was very grateful to her for everything.

Sandra was a dear, loving woman who cared more about other people than herself. First in her life was God, second were others, and last was herself. She lived a godly life, and Charlene admired her for it. In physical appearance, the two of them had many similarities. Sandra's brownish-blonde hair dangled at the edge of her shoulders, and her green eyes twinkled in the sunlight the same way Charlene's did. From afar, they could definitely be identified as sisters.

Charlene's flight to Calgary was arranged for the following day. She had already packed everything she needed and would use this time to rest and mentally prepare herself for the surgery.

Her nervousness continued to weaken her to a point where she would rather die. However, every time she felt scared, she repeated verses from the Bible to strengthen her.

As the next day rolled around, she did just that as she hastily maneuvered her Durango into the direction of the airport. In barely a murmur, she said, "The Lord Himself goes before you and will be with you; He will never leave you nor forsake you. Do not be afraid; do not be discouraged" (Deuteronomy 31:8, NIV). God's promise was a comfort to her, and despite her fear, he would be there each step of the way. That's why life was called a journey.

The time passed slowly as she patiently waited for her flight. When she finally boarded the small plane, she stopped for a brief moment as she looked behind and whispered under her breath, "I love you, Todd." As she stared at the vast beauty around her, the night before instantly replayed in her memory.

She had gone to the hospital to be with Todd. Overwhelmed by her situation, she had cried her heart out. She was afraid to have a brain tumor, and she was afraid to have it removed. The line was drawn in the middle; either way she could possibly die.

Firmly, she had held Todd's hand in her own as she uttered, "I am so scared, Todd. I don't know what to do. I trust God; I really do. But I can't help but wonder that I might die. I am not brave like Nate was, but I promise that I will continue to trust in God. You take care, Todd."

She had adjusted her posture as she rubbed his strong hand against her face. For Todd and the baby's sake, she would be brave.

Facing the plane that would fly her to meet her fears, she gripped her purse tightly as she slowly walked inside it.

As the dragging hours passed, she finally arrived in Calgary and was in the cozy comfort of her sister's home. Sandra and Matt's house was elegant. It was a two-story structure with a beautiful scenic view from the back.

As the glow from the fireplace in the living room brought forth warmth throughout their home, Charlene stood by the windowsill, staring out into the misty fog that overwhelmed the city. Her mind was in a daze as her thoughts drifted into days past. The memories of when she was once sixteen swirled through her brain. It was about this time of year that nearly twenty years ago Todd had tried to capture her attention with little success.

For a brief moment, the past suddenly evaporated as Sandra ambled toward her. "Are you okay, Charlene?"

"Yes, I'm fine. I was just thinking about when I was sixteen. Do you remember how disastrous my first date with Nate was?" Charlene giggled as her mind dove back into former years.

"Do I ever. Todd was so in love with you that he tried to make you jealous by taking me out on a date. He ended up taking me to the exact same restaurant you and Nate were at on purpose."

"And you thought Todd was interested in you."

"Yes, well, I didn't realize how much Todd really cared for you, Charlene. It's hard to believe you were never fond of him back then."

"I think it was because Todd was so different from Nate. Todd would tease me all the time. He used to pull on my pigtails or do some other goofy thing to get my attention. And Nate, well, he was so gentle and sweet, quite opposite from Todd actually." Charlene rubbed her eyes as she listened intently to her sister's response.

"I think Todd was always jealous of Nate. Nate had a way about him that always captivated you."

"You know, sometimes I still miss Nate. I love Todd dearly, but I can't help but wonder what my life would have been like if Nate was still here," Charlene paused for a brief moment. "Sandra, do you think I rushed into getting married to Todd?"

"Well, you love Todd, don't you?"

"Of course I do. But maybe if I hadn't married him, he wouldn't have lost his job or been in an accident. I feel as though I could have prevented all that has happened." Unexpectedly, the tears gently descended Charlene's face as if somehow it was her responsibility that Todd was dying.

"No, Charlene, you couldn't have prevented what happened. It's not your fault at all. God has a special plan for you."

"You're right. I am worried over something I can't change," Charlene said with a hopeful tone, even though she felt more hopeless than ever.

Although Charlene said that Sandra was right, deep inside she still felt torn and helpless. Finally, the barrier broke, and the tears flooded from her eyes. "Why is God making me go through this journey? I don't understand."

Softly, Sandra responded, "Oh, Charlene, God is not responsible, and he certainly is not the one to blame."

"Well, he took Nate away from me."

"And God gave you Todd. He hasn't left you alone to suffer through this. God is there for you; he is going to walk beside you the whole way. But you have to let him. You are going to get through this. I know you are. Charlene, you are a strong woman, and with God's help, you can face this. We can only overcome the battles in life with God's strength. It is through him that we conquer everyday struggles. Believe me, I know."

Charlene wiped her teary, green eyes as she focused on the beautiful prairie hills that surrounded them. Sandra was right. It wasn't God's fault.

Without delay, Sandra continued, "In fact, he hurts when we hurt. God wants to help us through. He doesn't want to stand and watch us continue to ache; he wants to help us. If only we understood how much God cares for us. His very touch is the miracle that changes our lives—he heals us with his unfailing love," Sandra gently spoke as she embraced her overwhelmed sister. "It is going to be okay. I promise."

"How do you know?"

"I have faith."

As the next day pronounced it's coming, the sun brightly shone through the glass windows of the classy home. Today was the day.

When Sandra and Charlene finally arrived at the Calgary hospital, the nervousness dug a pit deep inside Charlene's stomach. She was so afraid. What if this was the last day she had to live? As she waited, the thought continuously spun through her head.

Slowly, she uttered, "Please, God, be with me. I need you."

Sobbing endlessly, Sandra comforted her frightened sister. Finally, the dreaded time arrived. As three nurses wheeled her away, she whispered a prayer, "God, be with me and protect me. 'The Lord Himself goes before you and will be with you; He will never leave you nor forsake you. Do not be afraid; do not be discouraged' (Deuteronomy 31:8, NIV). Please don't leave me, God. I am very afraid."

After four hours of waiting, Sandra was becoming helpless. She loved her baby sister so much and prayed every minute Charlene was in the operating room. Finally, Dr. Smith ambled toward her. Her heart was pounding faster than a drum as he halted in front of her. *Is Charlene okay? Say something*, Sandra thought as she impatiently waited for him to speak.

"She's fine. She is completely fine," he declared, the light revealing his dimples.

"May I see her?" Sandra asked, the uneasiness subduing from inside.

"Yes, you may. Follow me."

As he guided her to Charlene's room, she softly murmured, "Thank you, God. You are so amazing," she began as she blinked back the overwhelming tears. "Thank you for protecting Charlene, God. Continue to show your compassion toward her as she faces each day. Amen."

As Sandra walked inside the dark room, she noticed Charlene sleeping soundlessly. Her head was wrapped in a white bandage, and her beautiful blond hair had been shaved off.

Lowering herself into a chair, Sandra folded her hands and continued to pray. Gradually, Charlene inched her eyes open to witness Sandra bowing her head in prayer. *I wish I were close to God the way Sandra is. I mean, I love God, but I don't always follow him the way I should. I want to desire him with all of my heart, but sometimes, I fail. How can Sandra make it seem so easy when I find it so hard?*

Slowly, Sandra lifted her head and smiled. Grabbing Charlene's hand, she gripped it tightly. "You are going to be okay, Charlene. God is good."

Charlene stared at her sister for a moment, and as the curiosity tore at her for an answer, she bravely asked, "Sandra, are you close to God? Every time I see you, you are either praying or showing God's love to other people. How do you do that?"

Sandra's face revealed a soft, light expression. "It's not always easy, but I have come to realize that God has to be your first and main priority, the center of your life. You have to love him with all of your heart, mind, and soul. God is the only one who can make you happy. Without God, there is no hope, no reason to live. God is our hope, the only reason to live. In Christ, you are made truly alive. But you have to be willing to let God take complete control of your life. You will no longer rule, but God will. You have to surrender. In the gospel Matthew, Jesus said, 'If anyone wishes to come after me, he must deny himself and take up his cross and follow Me. For whoever wishes to save his life will lose it; but whoever loses his life for My sake will find it. For what will it profit a man if he gains the whole world and forfeits his soul? Or what will a man give in exchange for his soul?' (Matthew 16:24–26, NASB). Each day I encounter situations that strengthen my walk with him. It is a lifetime journey. There is always room to grow."

Charlene felt like a young child asking her older sister for advice, yet something deep inside her soul urged her to continue the conversation.

"Do you think it is wrong to sometimes doubt if God is really there?"

A gentle smile appeared on Sandra's face as she attempted to answer her sister's question. "I think that God understands that we all have our days. We aren't perfect, and he doesn't expect us to be because we can't be. Satan begins to poke at us, and we lose faith. Even though we sometimes wonder if he exists and give up on him, he never gives up on us. It is comforting to always know that he is there no matter what the circumstance may be. But we have to understand that we do live by faith. In the Bible, it says, 'For we walk by faith, not by sight' (2 Corinthians 5:7, NASB). We have to believe and have faith that he exists because we can't see him. It is the way God works. But we have to remember not to depend on our feelings. That is when we get ourselves into lots of trouble. Our feelings change day to day. One day you may feel really close to God while the next, you are lonely and confused. We have to have faith and stand firm in our faith, not in our feelings," Sandra paused a brief moment. "'In Him we were also chosen, having been predestined according to the plan of Him who works out everything in conformity with the purpose of His will, in order that we, who were the first to hope in Christ, might be for the praise of His glory' (Ephesians 1:11–12, NIV). He already has a reason and a plan for everything, Charlene. You just have to believe and trust that he does. He knows why you are going through all of this. He really does, and he truly cares and loves you. Only God can complete you. Nothing else in this life can fill your emptiness. Like I said before, he is the miracle that we've all been praying for."

Sandra sounded so sure of herself. The words she said repeatedly played over in Charlene's mind. 'God has to be your first priority.' That was it. God had never been first in Charlene's life. She admitted that she had continuously laid aside her Bible. All she ever did was ask God for direction and guidance, yet she rarely ever did read his Word. At this moment, however, all she longed for was to be close to him.

Slowly, Charlene asked, "Sandra, do you have a Bible on hand?"

Sandra instantly grabbed her purse and pulled out a shiny, black, miniature Bible. She gently placed it in Charlene's hands. Flipping the crisp pages, Charlene opened the precious book and silently read, "The most important one," answered Jesus, "is this: 'Hear, O Israel, the Lord our God, the Lord is one. Love the Lord your God with all your heart and with all your soul and with all your mind and with all your strength.' The second is this: 'Love your neighbor as yourself.' There is no commandment greater than these" (Mark 12:29–31, NIV).

Everything began fitting into place. She needed God more than she had ever known.

A yearning deep inside urged her to continue her search through the Bible. After turning to John 15, she filled her hungry soul.

> "I am the true vine, and My Father is the vinedresser. Every branch in Me that does not bear fruit, He takes away; and every branch that bears fruit, He prunes it so that it may bear more fruit. You are already clean because of the word which I have spoken to you. Abide in Me, and I in you. As the branch cannot bear fruit of itself unless it abides in the vine, so neither can you unless you abide in Me.
>
> I am the vine, you are the branches; he who abides in Me and I in him, he bears much fruit, for apart from Me you can do nothing. If anyone does not abide in Me, he is thrown away as a branch and dries up; and they gather them, and cast them into the fire and they are burned. If you abide in Me, and My words abide in you, ask whatever you wish, and it will be done for you. My Father is glorified by this, that you bear much fruit, and so prove to be My disciples.

> Just as the Father has loved Me, I have also loved you; abide in My love. If you keep My commandments, you will abide in My love; just as I have kept My Father's commandments and abide in His love. These things I have spoken to you so that My joy may be in you, and that your joy may be made full.
>
> "This is My commandment, that you love one another, just as I have loved you. Greater love has no one than this, that one lay down his life for his friends. You are My friends if you do what I command you. No longer do I call you slaves, for the slave does not know what his master is doing; but I have called you friends, for all things that I have heard from My Father I have made known to you. You did not choose Me but I chose you, and appointed you that you would go and bear fruit, and that your fruit would remain, so that whatever you ask of the Father in My name He may give to you. This I command you, that you love one another.
>
> John 15:1–17 (NASB)

The words from the passage comforted her and made her realize that Sandra was right. God had to be first in her life. She was just so grateful to him for loving her even though she made many mistakes. Indeed there was a reason for every mishap that stumbled into her life.

The successful surgery gave her hope to continue on in life. She had overcome one battle and was ready to face other challenges that came her way.

Recuperating her strength, Charlene was finally released from the hospital's quarters after one long week. She had been more tired during her stay in the hospital, eating unpleasant food and residing in an environment that seemed so lonely. Everyone being sick around her was not a welcoming thought. She felt for the other people who were there, some who were too ill to talk, while others couldn't even move.

As she staggered out of the building, Sandra directed her to where her blue Corvette was parked. The short drive to the airport was filled with a misty silence.

Immediately upon arriving, Charlene hugged Sandra and softly whispered, "I am going to miss you, Sandra. Thank you for continuously praying for me. I know my struggles are not over, but I feel refreshed and my spirit is set anew. God is truly good."

Hollering behind her as she strode up the walkway to the building, she yelled, "Come and visit me soon."

After she boarded the plane and was settled into a comfortable seat, she solemnly prayed, "Thank you, God, for providing me with protection. I am truly sorry for doubting you sometimes. It's not that I don't believe you exist; it's just that sometimes I lose faith that you really care for me. I guess it is partially because everything seems to go wrong in my life. But I thank you for giving me the strength to endure and press on. It's not always easy to believe, but I know you are always there for me. Please be with this precious life inside me. Amen."

She tenderly rubbed her belly that was beginning to take shape. She was three and a half months along, and she just prayed that the little one inside her would continuously be protected.

Upon arriving in Edmonton, she carried her luggage to her black Durango and hopped inside. Steering her vehicle through the crowded streets, she finally reached the hospital. She didn't really want to be inside another lonesome infirmary, but the urge to see Todd overpowered the striking thought.

When she strode into his room, her eyes popped wide open. Scanning the area desperately, she couldn't believe it. Todd was gone. What happened? Where was he? Had he died? She instantaneously pushed the unwelcoming thought away as she searched for him. Frantically, she marched to the front desk.

As she choked on her tears, it was difficult to verbalize the words.

However, after sniffling away the pain and anxiety, she managed to quietly utter, "Where is Todd Carter? He used to be in room 307 on the second floor."

The kind lady gently explained, "He was moved up to the fourth floor. He needed more attention and care than what could be provided for him on this floor. He is now in room 219."

After thanking the sweet woman, Charlene scurried up the long, winding stairs to the fourth floor and directed her steps into Todd's new room. There he was lying soundless and peaceful on a soft bed in the corner.

"I love you, Todd. Don't go. I am okay. The brain tumor is gone. Dr. Smith said I healed faster than normal. I am going to be here for you, Todd. You are everything to me. You'll be okay. Hold on, darling. Hold on," she whispered as she sat down next to him on the hospital bed.

Clutching his hand, she cuddled close to him. She instantly fell fast asleep next to him as she gradually closed her tired eyes.

Awakening the next morning, she panicked not remembering where she was. Bouncing up, she jerked her body upwards as everything sank in. She was at the hospital next to Todd; everything was okay. Gradually, she leaned over and kissed his forehead. She swiftly arose to her feet and brushed her fingers over her hair that was beginning to grow back. Quickly, she grabbed her cute green hat from off the floor and placed in on her head.

Unequivocally, she briskly scampered downstairs to the café. As she ordered her food, she couldn't help but notice a sign that said Help Wanted. Ideally, if she worked here, she would be very close to Todd.

Just then, a petite, tall woman sweetly asked, "Can I help you, ma'am?"

"Yes, I was wondering if I could apply for a job. It says here that help is wanted."

"Well, if you could just fill out this form and bring it back to me as soon as you are finished, I'll have a look at it. In the meantime, would you like to order anything?" The lady was wearing black flannel pants and a white blouse. Slowly, she handed Charlene an application.

"Yes, that would be great. I'll get a coffee and a blueberry muffin," Charlene responded as she grabbed the white piece of paper and gripped it tightly in her hand.

"Is that everything? That comes to $3.75," the woman said as she passed Charlene her food and drink.

After paying, Charlene immediately retired to a green booth in the corner and began filling out the application. As soon as she could find a job, the better off she would be. Munching on her delicious, moist muffin and sipping her hot coffee, she quickly scratched in the required information. After she finished eating, she slowly ambled up to the front counter.

The sweet woman scanned the sheet over and quietly said, "I don't usually do this, but I am in desperate need of assistance. I only have one other worker. You are hired. Can you start work sometime next week?"

Shocked at the immediate hiring, Charlene hesitated, "Yes, well, of course. That sounds fantastic. Thank you."

"Let's say next Wednesday at nine in the morning?"

"That sounds perfect," Charlene replied. As Charlene sauntered back to her booth, she noticed Marcy sitting there alone.

"Hello, Marcy. Do you mind if I sit here with you?" Charlene kindly asked.

"Of course not. Have a seat." Marcy motioned for Charlene to sit down.

As Charlene lowered herself onto the comfortable green cushion, Marcy exclaimed, "Charlene, he remembers! Rick knows who I am. He's coming home today."

The tears trickled down her sweet face as she continued, "I just cannot believe it. God is so amazing. You know, he works in the most unexpected ways."

"I am so happy for you, Marcy. God answered our prayers." Charlene could not help but feel a little bit sorry for herself because Todd was not yet awake.

"Well, how are things, Charlene? How's Todd?" Marcy asked.

Sharing about her brain tumor and how she overcame the surgery, Charlene emptied her burdens one by one as she spilled her feelings out to her friend. She knew that Marcy would somewhat understand what she was going through. The pain agonized her deeply, and she was relieved to have somebody to talk to. Comforting Charlene, Marcy reassured her that everything would be all right, even though she didn't know if it would be. She put her complete faith in God that he would be there for Charlene no matter what. Besides, he knew what would happen, and he was in control of whatever lay ahead.

Unexpected News

The days swiftly passed one day at a time. It had been five months since Todd's tragic accident, and there was no sign of healing whatsoever.

The baby, who was growing inside her, was healthy every time Charlene went in for her regular appointments. She was so grateful to God. He must have known she could not handle any more hardship. Right now, she needed all the joyous uplifts in life to strengthen her during this difficult journey.

Her job at the hospital was decent, and Charlene was enjoying every minute of it. The sweet, kind lady she had talked with earlier was her boss. Her name was Dorothy, and she was always very compassionate. Charlene had no problem getting along with her.

In Charlene's spare time, while she waited with Todd in his room, she began wondering what to name their child. In three months, the baby would be due, and she couldn't just call him or her a baby forever.

Finally, she decided on Nathaniel, which means "gift of God" if it was a boy, and for a girl, Grace, which means "favor or blessing."

At this point in her life, her days were filled with many trips back and forth to the hospital for work as well as to be with Todd. Dr. Jens still didn't expect Todd to wake up but rather assumed that sooner or later he would be pronounced brain dead. Charlene tried her hardest not to think that way. Instead, she focused on the slight possibility that he may survive. God heard her prayers, and she knew that if it was his will, he would answer them. Truly all she wanted was for Todd to wake up from his devastating case of a coma, yet she was willing to accept whatever God had in store for her no matter how hard or difficult it would be.

One morning, in the early spring days of April, she received a brief letter from The Children's Aid Foundation concerning her niece's whereabouts. Peering inside the sticky, white envelope that was addressed to her, Charlene gently pulled out a piece of paper. Slowly, the striking news sank inside her mind.

Dear Mrs. Carter,

We have tried to contact you for several months now. Todd's sister, Martha Riley, passed away a few months ago. You are her daughter's only living relative. Martha's husband died several years ago due to a work-related accident, and Aimee, her fifteen year-old daughter, has been residing at the orphanage since her mother's passing. We are asking of you to please consider taking this child into your own custody. Please respond to our request immediately, so we can make further arrangements. Thank you in advance for your attention. We eagerly wait for your response to the need of this young child.

Sincerely,
The Children's Aid Foundation

As she wondered what kind of a life could be led without parents, she wasn't sure what to do. Should she take full responsibility of the child? It wouldn't be right or fair to just leave the girl in the orphanage when she could provide a life outside of it. What was God leading her to do?

Finally, she reached a verdict as she pulled out a clean, blank sheet of paper from the kitchen drawer. Processing ideas of what to say through her tired mind, she carefully recorded her thoughts onto the paper before her.

To The Children's Aid Foundation,

I have recently received your letter in regards to stabilizing a home for a young teenage girl named Aimee Riley. Willingly, I welcome her to come and live with me in my home. I am very sorry to hear that her mother has passed away. I sympathize with the young girl, as I, too, know what it is like to lose those you love. As these are the years when she needs a mother the most, I agree to take full custody of the child. Thank you for giving me this wonderful opportunity.

Sincerely yours,
Charlene Carter

Being a mother required a lot of skill; she would be provided with lots of practice before having her own.

Excitedly, she arranged the pieces of furniture around in one of their small guest rooms. She wanted Aimee to feel at home and have a place of her own.

After a long period of shoving the dressers here and there, Charlene unhurriedly staggered to the soft, black leather couch in the living room. Retiring for a nap, Charlene fell into a deep, comforting sleep. It was good to rest and refill her energy. The tiring days ahead would be packed with arrangements for her new welcomed guest.

As she dozed off, she dreamed about Todd. He was running toward her with his burly arms welcoming her into his embrace. Just as his chest softly caressed her sweet face, she suddenly awoke startled. Frantically, she sat up and gazed at the bountiful rain that pounded against the glass windows as it descended from the grayish, white sky. Striding to the now blurred window, she stared in awe at the beautiful rain tinkling down the side of the house.

The past suddenly seeped into her thoughts as her wedding with Nate replayed in her mind.

It had been on a cool, autumn day. As the rain gently drizzled over the earth, the colorful leaves had twirled through the air until they softly fell onto the muddy ground.

When the clouded sky had finally withheld its sprinkle of tears, Nate and Charlene had swiftly walked down the church steps together, hand in hand. As they descended the wet, slippery sidewalk, Charlene had accidentally stepped on her white, flowing dress. She rapidly traced over her steps and tried to balance the unevenness in her coordination. As she quickly covered up her embarrassment, she skimmed her guests' faces, hoping none of them took notice of the tiny tear at the bottom of her gown. Not realizing it, she had proudly walked onto the muddy, slimy dirt off to the left of the cement sidewalk. Suddenly, she lost her balance and dove into the wet, damp dirt, inevitably pulling Nate down with her. As everyone began laughing, Nate just grinned at her and affectionately kissed her lips.

Although it had been an embarrassing wedding, she couldn't help but laugh about it now.

Smiling softly, she stepped outside the door and onto the open deck and let the rain sprinkle over her. It felt like God was showering her with his never-ending love as the rain tenderly touched her skin. Gazing up at the clouded, cotton-like sky, the droplets lightly slid down her face as she prayed.

"God, you are so miraculous. Thank you for everything you have done in my life. I have been so focused on what has been going on that I have forgotten to thank you for everything. I want to open my heart to you and read the Bible daily. God, you truly are everything to me. This rain, it is such a blessing. It is a beautiful part of your marvelous creation. I thank you for it. Amen."

After feeling God's presence and peace restore her, she slowly sauntered inside the warm, cozy home that awaited her. Instantly, she directed her tiny steps into her yellowish-brown bedroom and supported herself against the side of her bed. Reaching for her Bible, she grabbed it off the nightstand and filled her aching soul with God's Holy Word.

> Do you not know? Have you not heard? The Everlasting God, the Lord, the Creator of the ends of the earth does not become weary or tired. His understanding is inscrutable. He gives strength to the weary, and to him who lacks might He increases power. Though youths grow weary and tired, and vigorous young men stumble badly, yet those who wait for the Lord will gain new strength; they will mount up with wings like eagles, they will run and not get tired, they will walk and not become weary.
>
> Isaiah 40:28–31 (NASB)

This was a deep encouragement to her as she scooted to the bathroom to get ready for bed. After she finished, she sank into her warm, welcoming bed and stretched the covers over her ice-cold bare feet.

It had been a day full of many exciting surprises, despite the fact that almost everything lately had reversed and gone the unexpected path of what seemed to be the worst. In a couple of strenuous weeks, Charlene would be the loving, caring mother of a fifteen-year-old girl. God had a reason and a plan for everything. Time would tell what he had in store.

Life carried on and with it carried the hope and fullness that everyday brought forth. It was a time to renew her faith and grow closer to God. Now was when she longed for God to be her stronghold. Her heart and soul yearned for him; she desired more than anything to strengthen her relationship with him. During this doubtful time, she needed God to keep her strong. He was the only one that would be there for her every minute of the day, to comfort her and lift her up.

It was a journey, a hard, discouraging journey. But God would walk her through it, and she completely trusted that he would.

Aimee Arrives

Tiring and unbearable days accompanied the long weeks of preparing for Charlene's niece, Aimee. It had been two weeks now since Charlene had replied to the Children's Aid Foundation, and she hadn't received any news yet to when Aimee would be arriving.

Nearing the end of April, information was finally delivered to Charlene containing details of Aimee's arrival. Quickly, she tore open the envelope and excitedly read what it had to offer.

> Dear Mrs. Carter,
>
> Recently we received your letter, and we are very grateful to you for your hospitality. We highly recognize your compliance for offering a stable home for your niece, Aimee. She is a vibrant, strong-willed girl full of life. She desperately needs a mother who will teach her discipline and the principles of life. We are very thankful that you are so willing to take on such a responsibility. She should be arriving in two days, no later. Please pick her up on April 19 at 10:00 a.m. at the Edmonton Airport. We

thank you again for inviting her to be a new addition to your family. She is very excited to meet you.

Sincerely,
The Children's Aid Foundation

As the two days quickly passed, Charlene was becoming nervous. What if Aimee did not like or respect her? What would she do if that were the case?

Early in the morning on the day of Aimee's arrival, Charlene summarily directed her slick, black Durango to the south side of town. After she parked her vehicle, she strode up the cement walkway.

The early morning heat was already steaming through the streets of Edmonton. Inside the airport, the coolness from the air-conditioning refreshed her inside out, and it felt wonderful to be trapped within the blowing cold airs reach.

Thrilled with anticipation to finally meet her niece, Charlene stood by the sizeable glass window and skimmed the hazy, pink sky for Aimee's plane.

Finally, she spotted a tiny airplane in the smog that slowly unveiled as it neared. Swooping to the ground, the aircraft finally wheeled its way to a halt. The first person off the plane was a tall, old man with a black cane in his left hand. His scruffy white, gray beard dangled from beneath his chin.

After a group of middle-aged people descended the ramp, a girl with long, blond hair and beautiful baby-blue eyes casually strutted down, following the rest of the crowd to retrieve her luggage.

Promptly, Charlene ambled toward the beautiful girl and courageously asked, praying that God had led her to her niece, "Are you Aimee Riley?"

The girl immediately nodded as Charlene proceeded to make conversation. "I am your Aunt Charlene, your Uncle Todd's wife. How was your flight?"

Shrugging her shoulders and rolling her eyes, Aimee glared at her aunt as if she were too cool to even be standing next to her. This was going to be more of a challenge than Charlene had expected it to be.

"Why don't I take your bags?" Charlene offered.

Slowly, the girl handed her aunt the two bags that she firmly gripped in her hands.

"I thought we would go home, and I can show you around, where your room will be and all," Charlene verbalized.

Aimee stared blankly at her aunt with her right hand on her hip. *This girl has nothing to say, no mind to speak of. Maybe she is just tired or shy,* Charlene considered as they marched outside of the well-built structure to her Durango waiting outside.

Silence filled the ride home as Charlene pulled up onto the long driveway. As she turned off the ignition, Aimee hurriedly climbed out of the parked vehicle and reached for her bags that were lying on the floor. Quickly, Charlene guided Aimee up the recently swept concrete steps and swung the front antique door open. The country furnished home was decorated with many rustic cream cans painted with beautiful sceneries. In the front entry, a milk can displayed a picture of Anne of Green Gables. Anne was staring in amazement at the vast beauty around her as Matthew Cuthbert steered the horse and buggy along the narrow road.

Slowly, Aimee followed Charlene through the living room into a long, stretched hallway containing three bedrooms, one off to the left and the other two off to the right.

"Here is your room, Aimee. Why don't you unpack your things while I make lunch, all right?" Charlene declared.

Unhurriedly, the slim girl ambled into her fine decorated room and tossed her bags on top of the turquoise and brown comforter that flowed like a fountain across her bed.

When Aimee finally finished unloading the little that she had, she leisurely strolled into the now messy kitchen. The counters were overflowing with scattered condiments and loaves of bread. Immediately, Aimee retired her aching body into a welcoming cushioned chair and gulped a bite of her peanut butter and jelly sandwich down.

"Dear, we are going to pray first. God has provided us with a wonderful meal. We should be very thankful."

Aimee rolled her baby-blue eyes and flipped her long, blond hair behind her shoulder. "Why? There is nothing to be thankful for anyways," she snapped.

"As long as you live in this house, we will pray before we eat. There are plenty of things to be thankful for," Charlene firmly stated.

"Well, why should I be thankful to God for letting my parents and the rest of my family die? Now I am stuck with you!" the sharp-tongued girl yelled.

Charlene didn't always understand why God took away loved ones, but God had his reasons, some to be unknown while others were to be revealed in his timing. That was all for God to know, not her.

"Go to your room right now. I will not tolerate this kind of behavior," Charlene firmly declared.

The girl glared at her with fiery burning hate in her eyes. "I don't have to listen to you. You are not my mother."

Calmly, Charlene tried to maintain her temper as she said, "I don't suppose you talked to your mother this way. It is very disrespectful, and I do not approve of such rude behavior."

Instantly, Aimee stood up and stormed off to her bedroom. "I hate you! Living here is worse than the orphanage!" Aimee screamed.

Crying softly, Charlene cupped her face in her tiny hands. At the time being, she did not understand why God wanted her to take care of Aimee. Was it to show the young girl the love and kindness that she so much longed for? Aimee lacked so much, and Charlene hoped she could offer her what she needed. But most of all, Charlene prayed that she could somehow lead her to what was the greatest gift of all, a relationship with Jesus Christ.

Bowing her head, she silently prayed, *Dear God, I thank you for this wonderful food that you have provided. Please give me the strength and energy to deal with this spirited young girl. 'God is our refuge and strength, a very present help in trouble'* (Psalms 46:1, NASB). *Please, God, enable me to love Aimee. I know that is what she needs right now, love. Thank you for everything, God. Amen.*

After Charlene finished her scrumptious tuna sandwich, she slowly tottered to Aimee's bedroom and knocked firmly on the wooden framed door. To her surprise, there was no answer. Gently, Charlene screeched the creaky door open. Blowing swiftly with the brisk breeze that filled the bright-yellow room, the brown, velvet curtains swayed back and forth. As the rich, green leaves from outside fluttered through the open window onto the brown, fluffy carpet, Charlene noticed all of Aimee's belongings were no longer on the dresser. Panicking, Charlene didn't know what to do. Where was Aimee, and where had she run off to?

Teenage Trouble

Worry replaced the harshness in Charlene's voice as she scurried outside yelling, "Aimee, where are you? I didn't mean to get so upset. I am so sorry. I do understand how you feel. You are angry that everyone you love has passed on. But don't be angry with God; it does no use. He is the only one who can help you through everything in life. You just have to trust him."

After an hour of driving continuously up and down the streets, Charlene reversed her Durango into the steady direction of home. Where could have the girl gone in such little time?

Whispering a prayer under her breath as she parked her vehicle on the driveway, Charlene cried, "God, be with Aimee. Please guide me to where she is. Amen."

As Charlene frantically scampered up the walkway, she heard chaotic noise echo in the spacious home. Striding inside the cool abode, Charlene scanned the living room and then fixed her eyes on the kitchen. To her astonishment and relief, Aimee was frenetically searching through the cupboards.

"What are you doing? Are you hungry?" Charlene managed to calmly ask.

Dismay echoed in Aimee's loud, boisterous voice as she answered, "You weren't supposed to come back yet."

Aimee had had this all planned. She had been hiding out in the backyard beneath her open window, waiting patiently until Charlene overworked herself to a stage of anxiety. When Charlene had left in search of her, she had made her escape back into the house to retrieve supplies before she actually ran away.

"You were planning to leave again, weren't you, Aimee?" Charlene softly asked.

"So what if I was? I hate it here. It's like a jail where I have to obey all these strict, dumb rules," Aimee barked.

"I really want you to stay, but it is your choice. Just keep in mind that there are rules that you have to abide by. Didn't your mother have rules?" Charlene inquired.

"If my mom wasn't high from drugs or alcohol, she was gone, and I was left alone. I did whatever I pleased," Aimee proudly announced. The truth became known. She had always been a willful child because no one had protected her by giving her boundaries to stay within.

"I want you to know that I would be more than happy for you to stay here with me. My rules are very simple. Respect is important," Charlene verbalized.

"You're like a communist dictator!" Aimee retorted.

Respiring in a deep, long breath, angriness overpowered Charlene. She was just about to say, *You little brat*! Nevertheless, something deep within her stopped the harsh words from flowing out of her mouth. She was the mother here, not the child. She had to behave properly and handle this situation in an appropriate manner.

"Well, aren't you going to send me to my room, again?" Aimee was in complete shock as her mouth dropped wide open.

Calmly, Charlene responded, "No, Aimee, I am not going to send you back to your room. This place is new to you, and I understand that it will take some time to come to know the rules. Are you hungry, dear?"

Nodding, a slight smile formed upon Aimee's face. "I am starving. Having supper early would be great."

After a filling dinner, Charlene and Aimee both decided to retire to their bedrooms to receive a full night's rest. The confusion that aroused that day caused both of them to fall asleep within seconds.

Tomorrow would be a full day, it being Aimee's first day at a new high school and all.

Slowly, the sun arose as it rested in the middle of the bright, blue sky. Stomping out of her room at eight o'clock in the morning, Aimee crisply shouted, "I am not going to school. If you make me, I will run away again."

The more Aimee showed off her true colors, the more Charlene wished she were the stuck up fifteen-year-old girl she had first met at the airport who had very little to say.

"You are going and that is final. We had this talk yesterday, Aimee, and I am not in the mood to have it again," Charlene firmly stated.

As the two quietly strode out of the country home, Aimee arrogantly declared, "You are a grandma. You look like one too. How old are you really? I'd say about sixty years of age if not older. I don't understand why that dumb orphanage wanted a grandma to take care of me. Usually old people start to shrivel and fall apart."

Charlene could not take it any longer. "Aimee Martha Riley, you will never talk like that again. Is that understood?" Charlene had lost it, and the words exploded out like lava erupting in an oozing volcano.

Aimee sat silently in the front seat next to her aunt on the way to school. As Charlene pulled her vehicle in front of the huge building that read: Eagle Ridge High School, Aimee slowly scrambled out.

"Thank you," Aimee said in an exaggerated tone.

Smiling softly, Charlene waved good-bye.

The quiet drive to the hospital was refreshing. The flowers along the road announced that spring was here. As the fragrant blossoms outlined the city, they gave her a rich feeling of hope, and she could not in any way deny that the Creator had made all things. The vast beauty declared that there was a God, and anyone who tried to denounce it was lying only to him or herself. It was a comfort to know that God not only made all things but also knew the specific purpose. There was a reason she was going through this journey, and ever since her heart-to-heart talk with Sandra, Charlene felt reassured that Christ was there for her through it all.

Immediately after entering the lonely infirmary, Charlene scurried to the café and set to work. Two hours into the tiring afternoon, Dorothy swiftly waltzed toward Charlene who was dealing with a grumpy, old man who was hard of hearing.

"I am not paying fifty-five dollars for a dinky muffin and tasteless cup of coffee," the aged man shouted.

"Sir, the amount is only five dollars and three cents."

"What? Did you say fifty-five dollars is sensible? I am taking my business elsewhere."

Interrupting, Dorothy gently placed a hand on Charlene's shoulder and whispered, "Charlene, I'll take over from here. Mr. Thomas from Eagle Ridge High School called. He would like to speak with you." She then turned to face the stubborn old man and sweetly said the required amount. The little man's face softened immediately as he handed Dorothy the money.

"Now that price is reasonable. Thank you, Miss Dorothy."

"You are very welcome, Mr. Tucker. I wish you all the best. I hope your wife gets better soon. Have a good day."

"I will, and you take it easy." The elderly man grabbed his coffee and muffin and disappeared up the steps.

Meanwhile, Charlene rapidly marched to the back of the restaurant and picked up the telephone. Burying the fear that burned deep within her, she sweetly said, “Hello. Yes, this is Charlene. She did what? I’ll be there right away.”

After hanging up, she quickly explained her dilemma to Dorothy.

“That is completely fine, Charlene. Just get back here as soon as you can.”

Thanking Dorothy for her compassion, Charlene bolted outside to her Durango and steered it into the direction of the school. Speedily, she swung her car door open and strode up the sidewalk, the anger boiling deep within her. Opening the heavy, glass door, she was still in shock that Aimee could arouse so much trouble. She really did not think that she could handle Aimee and her insolent attitude any longer. There was nothing that she could do to change Aimee except love and care for her in a motherly way. Suddenly, it hit her. Maybe that is what she needed after all, not an aunt but a mother, a kind, loving mother.

The Devised Plan

As Charlene briskly marched into the principal's office, she noticed Aimee sitting in the corner, secluded and isolated with her head hanging limply down. Immediately, Mr. Thomas arose from behind his desk and firmly uttered, "Aimee, you are free to leave. Your mother is—"

Interrupting rudely, Aimee bellowed, "She is not even close to being my mother. I don't even know her."

"I'm her aunt. She is living with me. Both of her parents died a while ago," Charlene corrected.

Mr. Thomas's face reflected a sympathetic expression as he firmly shook Charlene's hand. "I am very sorry to hear that."

After he dismissed them, Charlene ushered Aimee outside to the parking lot. "How could you do something so irresponsible, Aimee? What was going on inside your head?"

Shyly, the girl hid her face as she stared blankly at the rocky ground. "I don't know" was her smug reply.

"Tell me honestly, Aimee, did you seriously think you would get away with it?"

"I don't care, okay. I just wish you'd leave me alone."

Charlene tried to ignore the last disrespectful comment. "So you are going to tell me that you don't care that you stole fifty dollars worth of merchandise from a nearby grocery store?"

"Nope, I don't care a single bit. Why is it such a big deal anyways?"

"I am very disappointed in you. Aimee, don't you understand the consequences? You could go to jail for this. You committed a serious crime, and I am going to tell you right now that you will pay back what you stole five times over."

"I don't even have that much money."

"Well that doesn't matter because in your spare time, you will be working to earn that money. I suggest we find you a part-time job," Charlene instructed. "Staying busy should help keep you out of trouble," Charlene murmured under her breath.

The spring afternoon was accompanied with a rich breeze that showered the earth with a brisk, cool sensation. Beneath the hushed guidance of the wind, the firm trees swayed back and forth as they drove in silence back to the hospital.

As they entered the building, Charlene strictly said, "Aimee, I don't want you causing any more trouble. If you'd like, you can visit Uncle Todd. He is on the fourth floor in room 219. I am going to quickly find Dorothy and see if she still needs me. I'll come find you when I finish."

After taking a quick tour of the hospital, Aimee instantaneously retreated to her uncle's lonely room. Lowering herself into the stiff, unwelcoming chair, she slowly hesitated, "Uncle Todd, you seem so unlike Auntie Charlene. She is so bossy and irritating, and you are so sweet, gentle, and kind. I remember almost eight years ago when you came to visit my mom and me. I know I was only eight, but I will never forget it. I wish you had chosen somebody different to marry. There had to be someone else who would have been perfect for you. I mean there are millions of women to choose from. Why did you have to pick Auntie Charlene? I don't see anything special and unique about her. The only reason I am staying here is because I know you will wake up soon. I love you, Uncle Todd."

During the last few precious words, Charlene tiptoed into the still, quiet room. As a tiny tear descended Aimee's cheek, she ran to meet her aunt's embrace. The young girl just needed to be loved. For a long moment, the room was filled with a renewing peace.

Finally, Aimee asked, "Auntie, do you think Uncle Todd will be all right?" Charlene had never seen this side of Aimee before.

Tears brimmed over in Aimee's baby-blue eyes as she gazed at her aunt for an answer. Gently, Charlene said, "I believe he will. God is a miraculous God."

A slight smile appeared on Aimee's face as if it gave her a bit of hope to hold on to. Slowly, she whispered, "I hope you are right."

As the two departed from the hospital, they climbed inside the black, shiny Durango. It was becoming customary that when they drove a stale silence stung the air. Charlene supposed it was something she would just have to get used to.

Just as Charlene parked the vehicle on the cement driveway, Aimee quietly uttered, "I am sorry, Auntie Charlene." Had Charlene heard right? Was she apologizing? Before Charlene had a chance to reply, Aimee continued, "No, Auntie, I am sorry for everything, for yesterday and for today. What can I do to make it up to you?"

Charlene was completely stunned. What was going on? "An apology to Mr. and Mrs. Murphy would be a good start. Maybe you could arrange to work for them until you have paid off what you owe them."

"That sounds more than fair."

What had happened to Aimee? One minute she was self-centered and the next she was an entirely different girl.

Still shocked by Aimee's new attitude adjustment, Charlene ran the previous events through her head.

Suddenly, Aimee interrupted her thought life, "Auntie, I remember when Uncle Todd spent the entire summer with my mom and me in Detroit as if it were just yesterday. My dad died when I was six, and in a way, uncle Todd kind of replaced him. He taught me how to ride a bicycle and how to play baseball. During those childhood years when I really needed a daddy, he was always there."

Tranquility filled the muggy air for a brief moment until Aimee finally whispered, "I just hope that he is okay. Losing him would be like losing my father all over again."

"Would you like to pray for him? I know God would be more than happy to listen."

"No, I don't really know how, and besides, it's probably of no interest to him."

"If you would rather not, that is fine, but do you mind if I pray?"

Agreeing, Aimee and Charlene bowed their heads as Charlene murmured a soft little prayer for Todd, "God, please be with Uncle Todd. Please protect him and keep him safe. Thank you for my niece, Aimee. I am so very blessed to have her here with me. Be with her in whatever struggles she is facing. Amen."

A mischievous grin crept upon Aimee's face. T*hat's what you think, Auntie Charlene. You'll never even know the difference. You are way too old-fashioned to keep up with the new schemes teens have up their sleeves.* Aimee had nothing to worry about. Everything would work out to her advantage or so she thought.

Jesse

The next day was the beginning of a new month, the month of May. As the chirping of birds awoke Charlene, she hopped out of bed and quickly woke up Aimee. After a quick breakfast, they found themselves in the entryway ready to leave for the Murphy's store.

"If you don't mind, Auntie, I'll just walk there by myself," Aimee politely said as Charlene picked up the keys to her Durango. "It is such a gorgeous day, and the Murphy's grocery store is only a few blocks away. Don't worry, I know how to get there."

Slowly, Charlene hesitated noticing the sly twinkle in the girl's eye. For a brief moment, she stared at the floor and finally tucked her keys inside her purse. "All right, but no fooling around. I want you to go straight there, and I will pick you up in a little bit. Is that understood?"

Agreeing, Aimee flew out the door. She was wearing cute jean shorts and a turquoise, sequined tank top set off by a purple beaded necklace.

After ten minutes of non-stop running, she abruptly turned the corner and ducked behind some dark green bushes near the Murphy's store.

"Stacie, are you here?" Aimee whispered, gasping for breaths.

A mystifying person tucked behind the brush inched closer to Aimee as her hazelnut eyes glowed in the dim light.

"Did you bring me that stuff you promised?" Aimee hurriedly asked.

A girl with dead straight, reddish orange hair inched closer to the tree, so the sun skidded across her pale, white face. "Here, take it quick. I can see your aunt's Durango in the distance. You had better go." Stacie rapidly handed Aimee a brown paper bag.

Swiftly, Aimee shoved the bag into her purse, and before she was in view of her aunt, she nonchalantly sat down on a wooden bench outside of the Murphy's store. As the Durango crept closer, she stood up and scuttled toward it.

"Hi, Auntie. Mr. and Mrs. Murphy were so considerate. After I apologized, I offered to work for them, and I am scheduled for the next three Saturdays until I have paid everything off." A mysterious smirk stealthy tiptoed across Aimee's face as if she were hiding something deep within her. As she glanced down at her purse, she detected the brown paper bag peeking its head out.

Just then, Charlene curiously asked, "Aimee, what is inside that bag? I don't remember you having that before."

Quickly covering up her secret, Aimee blurted, "I just bought some gum. Would you like some?"

"Sure, that would be great." She reached inside the bag and pulled out a pack of cigarettes. Charlene directly shot a glance of disproval Aimee's way.

"Auntie, we have to go back. The clerk must have accidentally switched my gum with the man's purchase in front of me."

There was something about this situation that just didn't seem right. What was going on?

Without delay, Charlene reversed her vehicle back into the direction of the store. Upon arriving, Aimee jumped out and scurried up the sidewalk. As she entered the tiny building, she scanned the room for any sign of Mr. Murphy who had been there the day she had robbed the store. Thankfully the coast was clear. After the quick search, she immediately found a pack of gum and paid for it.

Returning to the car, she instantly gave her aunt a piece of the peppermint gum and jostled the box into the paper bag with her cigarettes.

My aunt is way too gullible. She will never find out that I kept the cigarettes, Aimee thought as a devious smile crawled upon her face.

Sunday arrived ever so quickly, and Charlene had begun her normal routine of occupying her mornings by attending church. As she quickly awoke Aimee, the smell that penetrated the room was absolutely horrifying. Suddenly, a box of cigarettes strewn on the floor came into clear view.

"Aimee, you said you returned those cigarettes yesterday. Why do you still have them?"

Aimee's face grew paler than ever. "I don't feel very well."

"I should say not. You have been smoking. I can tell by that awful scent. Get up. We are going to church in an hour. Be sure that you are ready." Charlene fanned the air with her hand as she picked up the white box. "We will talk about this later."

The church service had a good message. Charlene hoped Aimee was paying attention. Pastor Ray's sermon was based on a passage from the book of John. It was very intriguing.

> "Do not let your heart be troubled; believe in God, believe also in Me. In My Father's house are many dwelling places; if it were not so, I would have told you; for I go to prepare a place for you. If I go and prepare a place for you, I will come again and receive you to Myself, that where I am, there you may be also. And you know the way where I am going."
>
> Thomas said to Him, "Lord, we do not know where You are going, how do we know the way?"
>
> Jesus said to him, "I am the Way, and the Truth, and the Life; no one comes to the Father but through Me. If

you had known Me, you would have known My Father also; from now on you know Him, and have seen Him."

Philip said to Him, "Lord, show us the Father, and it is enough for us."

Jesus said to him, "Have I been so long with you, and yet you have not come to know Me, Philip? He who has seen Me has seen the Father; how can you say, 'Show us the Father'? Do you not believe that I am in the Father, and the Father is in Me? The words that I say to you I do not speak on My own initiative, but the Father abiding in Me does His works. Believe Me that I am in the Father and the Father is in Me; otherwise believe because of the works themselves. Truly, truly, I say to you, he who believes in Me, the works that I do, he will do also; and greater works than these he will do; because I go to the Father. Whatever you ask in My name, that will I do, so that the Father may be glorified in the Son. If you ask Me anything in My name, I will do it.

"If you love Me, you will keep My commandments. I will ask the Father, and He will give you another Helper, that He may be with you forever; that is the Spirit of truth, whom the world cannot receive, because it does not see Him or know Him, but you know Him because He abides with you and will be in you. I will not leave you as orphans; I will come to you. After a little while the world will no longer see Me, but you will see Me; because I live, you will live also. In that day you will know that I am in My Father, and you in Me, and I in you. He who has My commandments and keeps them is the one who loves Me; and he who loves Me will be loved by My Father, and I will love him and will disclose Myself to him."

Judas (not Iscariot) said to Him, "Lord, what then has happened that You are going to disclose Yourself to us and not to the world?"

Jesus answered and said to him, "If anyone loves Me, he will keep My word; and My Father will love him, and We will come to him and make Our abode with him. He

> who does not love Me does not keep My words; and the word which you hear is not Mine, but the Father's who sent Me.
>
> "These things I have spoken to you while abiding with you. But the Helper, the Holy Spirit, whom the Father will send in My name, He will teach you all things, and bring to your remembrance all that I said to you. Peace I leave with you; My peace I give to you; not as the world gives do I give to you. Do not let your heart be troubled, nor let it be fearful. You heard that I said to you, 'I go away, and I will come to you.' If you loved Me, you would have rejoiced because I go to the Father, for the Father is greater than I. Now I have told you before it happens, so that when it happens, you may believe. I will not speak much more with you, for the ruler of the world is coming, and he has nothing in Me; but so that the world may know that I love the Father, I do exactly as the Father commanded Me. Get up, let us go from here."
>
> John 14:1-31 (NASB)

Pastor Ray captivated the congregation's attention by emphasizing what Jesus was saying. "Jesus is telling his disciples that he is going to heaven to prepare a place for them. He says in verse 3, 'And if I go and prepare a place for you, I will come back and take you to be with Me that you also may be where I am.' He is comforting them. After Thomas finishes saying, 'Lord, we don't know where you are going, so how can we know the way,' Jesus explains that he is the only way, to the Father. Then from verse fifteen to thirty-one, Jesus promises the Holy Spirit. This is before the crucifixion." When Pastor Ray finished, he then prayed.

After the service, Charlene skimmed the familiar faces and noticed Marcy was there. That was very unusual since Marcy did not attend this church. Along the way to welcome her dear friend, a few people told her they were praying that God would be ever so near to her during this difficult time.

"Marcy, it is so good to see you. What are you doing here?"

"Emily, the young girl that sang special music, is my niece. I thought it would be nice to support her. She is going to be attending Bible school in New Zealand in the fall."

"That's right. I am glad that you are here. I was just thinking if you aren't too busy tomorrow you could come for coffee at my place at 10:00 a.m."

"Wonderful, I'll see you in the morning then."

As Monday announced it's beginning, the sun gleamed across the morning sky. It looked as though it was going to be a gorgeous day. Charlene eagerly bounced out of bed and pulled back her chin length blond hair into a ponytail. Her hair was growing back faster than she had expected. When she was finished getting ready, she quickly dropped Aimee off at Eagle Ridge High.

After arriving at home, she promptly grinded honey-roast coffee beans and dumped them into the coffee maker. When the shrill ring of a bell chimed, Charlene gladly welcomed Marcy inside the cool air-conditioned home. The heat from outside flooded through the open door and clashed with the cold air that was locked inside.

"Come on in, Marcy."

Leading her into the bright yellow kitchen, she motioned for Marcy to sit down as she retrieved the brewed coffee. As the two ladies sipped steamy hot cups of honey-roast coffee, Marcy sweetly asked, "How are you keeping, Charlene?"

"I am doing fine, and Aimee has adjusted quite well. Better than I expected, I suppose."

"I am sorry, but who is Aimee?"

"Aimee is my niece. Both of her parents died, and now she is living here with me."

"What is her last name?"

"Riley. Aimee Riley. Why do you ask?" Charlene inquisitively wondered.

"My son just recently met an Aimee Riley, and he is absolutely taken by her."

"Pardon me, you have a son? I did not know you had any children."

"Yes, Jesse is seventeen, and Karla is fifteen years old. I was married two years after you and I graduated from high school and had a baby the following year. I know, it must be weird to be only thirty-six and have such old kids."

Charlene was surprised, and her stunning green eyes reflected her astonishment. She *was* that old, and she was only pregnant.

"I just have this little one. He or she is kicking right now. Come feel," Charlene giggled. Slowly, Marcy placed a warm, soft hand on Charlene's stomach. She could feel the tiny baby squirming inside, and she rapidly jerked her hand away.

"He must be a feisty one. I am so happy for you, Charlene. Congratulations!" Marcy exclaimed.

A twinkle in Charlene's eye sparked as she immediately changed the subject. Pryingly, she asked, "How old is Jesse? What kinds of things has he mentioned about Aimee? You know, a mother must be inquisitive to keep her children within arm's reach."

Marcy smiled as she replied, "Jesse just turned seventeen, and he said he met a really pretty girl named Aimee Riley on the first day of school. He also said he has been trying to hangout with her and influence her as often as he can. He indicated that she has been hanging around with the wrong kind of crowd. Don't worry, Charlene, my boy is very careful."

A worried look suddenly flashed upon Charlene's face. "I am going to have to pray a lot, I guess. Did you say that Aimee has been hanging around bad influences?" Charlene questioned.

"That is what Jesse has said. He has said he tries to persuade her to hangout with him and his friends instead. I don't think she particularly likes when he stands firm in his faith. He desires to show God's love toward her and set an example of what true Christianity is. I can tell he becomes hurt when she ignores or mocks him for standing up. He is strong, and my prayer is that he will never give up. Speaking of God, I thoroughly enjoyed Pastor Ray's sermon yesterday. I was definitely touched by it."

"I hope Aimee was touched by it too. I know I was. I have been having problems with her. Yesterday I found out she has been smoking. I don't know how long this has been going on for, but I intend to find out. I have been praying for her constantly that God would work in her life. I just don't know what to do with her."

"Continue to pray for her and love her. I am sure she needs a mother who will really care for her. God will work out the rest."

After a moment, Charlene arose from the kitchen table and carried the dishes into the kitchen.

"Would you like to go for a walk?" Charlene kindly asked.

"Yes, I would. It is absolutely gorgeous outside," Marcy answered, her sweet voice ringing in the air.

As they strolled through the park, a gentle breeze swept over Charlene. The pink and purple flowers swayed, and the sweet fragrance enriched the air. The beautiful day sent shivers through her soul. It was as though God was gently whispering to her that he loved her and would always be there. No matter what life brought her way, he would be her safe haven.

Around three o'clock in the afternoon, Marcy quickly remembered she had to pick up Karla and Jesse from school. "If you'd like, we could pick up the kids together. Karla and Jesse both attend Eagle Ridge High. Why don't you come with me in my vehicle?"

As the two ladies walked home, the rich essence of God's presence and beauty showered over them. Every once in a while, the breeze would blow perfect, green leaves from the tree as they softly fluttered to the ground.

After arriving at Charlene's house, they swiftly climbed inside Marcy's white mini van and quickly drove to the school. As the van rolled around the corner, Charlene spotted Aimee in disbelief. There Aimee stood by the smoke pits with Stacie and three other kids from her class.

Sprinting from the vehicle, Charlene hastily made her way towards Aimee. The tears streamed down her sweet, gentle face. She felt like such a horrible mother. Even though Aimee recently came to live with her, she felt to some degree that this was all her fault. Clear as day, a cigarette was positioned in-between Aimee's lips.

"Aimee, I just don't believe you. Don't think you can fool me for one second, young lady. I know what you are up to. You have been acting different from who you really are," Charlene softly said as the tears continued to descend from her face. It was as if the rage inside her was all locked up and could not be released. At this point in time, all she could do was cry.

Off to her right, Charlene noticed a boy casually sauntering towards them. He was medium-sized build with a tall frame. Brown, short hair shaped his soft face, and piercing chocolate eyes sparkled beneath his brow.

"Aimee, what are you doing? Why are you smoking?"

Rolling her baby-blue eyes, Aimee placed her lit cigarette in an ashtray. "Jesse, I already told you I was going home after lunch because I felt sick. Why won't you just leave me alone?"

"You never called me, Aimee. I am very disappointed in you. Do you mean to tell me that you skipped class to smoke with your friends all day?" Charlene's harsh, stern tone of voice reflected the look of disproval on her face. "Aimee Martha Riley, you are grounded, and that is final. I told you yesterday before church I would deal with you. Now your punishment will be even more severe. I will not tolerate this kind of behavior."

Embarrassed by her aunt's reprimand, Aimee slowly trudged behind her to Marcy's vehicle.

Jesse and Karla were already in the back seat when Aimee squeezed in next to them. Quickly, Karla glared at Jesse as if to say, "What do you see in her? She is just plain trouble."

As Marcy pulled the mini van in front of the old-fashioned log home, Charlene sweetly uttered, "Thank you for such a wonderful visit. See you soon."

She marched into the house with Aimee following behind. She wasn't finished dealing with Aimee yet, and she prayed that God would give her the right words to say.

What's Going On?

The unbearable days slowly passed. It had been two weeks since the incident at Eagle Ridge High, and Aimee's temper was really getting out of hand.

"I hate you! I hate you! You are the worst. And I thought mothers were supposed to ruin everything. Well, aunts do too," Aimee puffed as she grabbed her pink, glittery purse.

"Aimee Martha Riley, don't you ever talk like that again. You just finished your grounding a few days ago. Would you like to come home after school on Monday and help with all the household chores?" Charlene calmly spoke as they hurried outside and climbed inside the recently cleaned Durango.

"I am used to it. Ever since I came here, all I ever do is come straight home after school. I have absolutely no privileges."

"You haven't earned any either," Charlene paused a brief moment as she steered the Durango into the path of the Murphy's store. "Obviously, I know more than you think. I called Mr. and Mrs. Murphy to ask how you had been doing at work last night. I just wanted to make sure you were staying out of trouble."

"That's your problem. You are so nosy," Aimee retorted.

Charlene knew she was not being overly strict when it came to Aimee stealing or smoking. Those things were wrong, just plain wrong. "Well, it is a good thing I was nosy. I found out that you had tricked me into believing you were working when you really weren't. That is negligent."

As Charlene guided her glossy Durango down the clean, paved road, she whispered a prayer under her breath, "Dear God, provide me with an internal peace. I am having such a difficult time dealing with Aimee, and I don't know what to do. Be with Todd. I love him dearly, and I know I cannot bear any more heartache. I need him to help me raise this baby, as well as, Aimee. Thank you for always listening and answering my prayers in your time. The answer is not always what I want to hear, but you always have a special reason and a purpose. Thank you. Amen."

Finally, Charlene rolled the car to a complete, abrupt stop, and they trudged up the sidewalk leading to the Murphy's general store.

"I can't believe you are making me do this," Aimee sputtered as Charlene opened the glass door to the tiny building.

Instantly, Aimee recognized the familiar voice as a tall man with fading dark blond hair stepped out from behind the counter. Charlene gently tugged on Aimee's arm and promptly marched toward the man.

"Morning, can I help you?" the sweet, elderly man verbalized.

"Yes, I am Charlene Carter. I spoke with you last night. This is my niece, Aimee."

"That is right. I remember now. Aimee, you came in here a couple of weeks ago and stole an assortment of merchandise." The man's wrinkly face remained calm, and he tried to conceal his fury.

"See, that is why we are here. Aimee, go on," Charlene articulated, motioning for Aimee to explain.

"Well, I…ah, I was wondering if I could work to pay off what I owe you. I promise I won't steal again." She took a deep breath before continuing, "I guess you both should know why I did it. My friends said I had to steal in order to be accepted by them. My aunt wanted me to confess right away. I lied to her and told her that you hired me, but really I was meeting my friend Stacie here. I know it sounds dumb, and I really am sorry. I know it was wrong. I was wondering if I could work for you until I have paid you back—"

Charlene hastily interrupted, "Aimee, you should never do anything to be accepted by other people. They are truly not your friends if they force you into doing things that are wrong."

"Calm down, ma'am. I will accept your proposal, Aimee. If it happens again, however, I'll be forced to bring the police into this. Do you understand?"

"Thank you, sir," Aimee replied as she accepted Mr. Murphy's handshake.

"You are very welcome, child. You will start tomorrow. Come here around three-thirty in the afternoon."

"See you tomorrow," Aimee shouted as she and Charlene exited the store.

When they arrived home, Charlene slipped out of the house for a leisurely stroll. Aimee had convinced her to go for a relaxing walk and to enjoy the gorgeous day. The Saturday sunshine beamed over her as she whisked her way around the park. She felt renewed, and she sensed a peace from God sprinkling over her weary soul. As she breathed in the fresh spring air, a verse from Pastor Ray's sermon a few Sunday's ago flashed in her mind. "Peace I leave with you; My peace I give to you; not as the world gives do I give to you. Do not let your heart be troubled, nor let it be fearful" (John 14:27, NASB). The peace she experienced at this moment was truly peace from God.

Listening to the birds sweetly chirping, she glanced up at the flawlessly blue, shimmering sky. Only God could make everything so perfect. Everything had its place.

Finally, Charlene slowly ambled back to her cozy, little home. As she screeched the front door open, she hollered, "Aimee, I am home."

There was no answer or reply, just a dead, horrifying silence.

"Aimee, are you here?" Charlene scanned the living room and slowly gazed at the recently swept floor. Aimee's black skateboarding shoes were nowhere in sight.

Panicking, Charlene dashed to the telephone. Frantically, she dialed Marcy's number. "Hello, Marcy, this is Charlene. I am so worried. I cannot find Aimee anywhere. I went for a walk in the park, and when I got back here, she was gone. I just don't know what to do. Is she with Jesse or Karla?" Charlene gasped for air.

"Calm down, Charlene. She is not over here. Jesse decided to walk to town about a half hour ago to get some fresh air, and Karla is at Tiffany's house," Marcy softly replied. Marcy and her family lived on a farm only ten minutes out of the city.

For a moment, silence nipped the air. Under her breath, Charlene whispered, "Dear Jesus, protect Aimee wherever she may be. I pray that you will show her the way, and that she will come to realize that you are the way, the truth, and the life. Be with her now. Amen."

As Charlene finished praying, she could hear the echo of shoes beating against the floor through the phone line. The thumping stopped, and she listened carefully to what was going on.

"Mom, they are in trouble. I have to phone the police," Jesse shouted.

"What's wrong, Jesse? Who is in trouble?" Marcy worriedly asked.

In the background, Charlene heard Marcy panicking as Jesse replied, "It's Aimee."

In that instant, Charlene dropped the phone, and it crashed to the ground. It felt like the entire world had stopped, the clock quit ticking.

As the tears endlessly poured from her eyes, she slowly picked up the receiver.

"Charlene, I think you had better come over here," Marcy uttered and instantly hung up the phone. Rapidly, Jesse snatched the phone and dialed the emergency number, responding with precise answers for all the required information.

"Maple Avenue. That's right. Bye." Jesse clicked the telephone in its rightful home and scampered back out of the house down the road. Just then, Charlene parked her Durango on the rocky gravel in front of the large farmhouse.

"What's going on? What happened to Aimee?" Charlene cried.

"Climb inside the van. Jesse informed the police that a car accident occurred on Maple Avenue. Aimee was involved in it," Marcy explained as they hopped inside the vehicle and raced down the road.

Upon arriving at the scene, Charlene noticed Jesse standing beside one of the crushed vehicles. The tears continuously poured down Charlene's face as she scampered out of the van and sprinted toward Aimee. She could hear the subtle tone of his voice as he softly spoke, "You are going to be all right. I promise. I won't let you go. I love you, Aimee." A tear slipped from the corner of his eye.

Charlene glanced inside the Corvette and saw long blond hair streaming from a young girl's face. It was Aimee sitting in the passenger seat. Slowly, Charlene prayed, "God, why? Why did this have to happen? Please protect her, God, please."

She stared at the hazy sky as the paramedics lifted Aimee out of the crunched Corvette. Slowly, the sun seeped behind the street houses that outlined the block, and a thick darkness happened to come upon them.

Charlene watched as Jesse walked away from where she was standing and began a conversation with one of the policemen. She was so lost in what was happening, and she instantly followed the young boy. As she intruded in on their conversation, Jesse immediately introduced her, "This is Aimee Riley's aunt, Charlene. Aimee is living with her."

"Charlene, you need to follow the ambulance to the hospital. There will be forms to sign to give your permission to operate on the girl."

Charlene forced the fumbled words out of her mouth as the agony bubbled up inside her, "All right, thank you, officer."

He nodded and promptly strutted away. Hurriedly, Charlene and Jesse returned to the mini van where Marcy waited impatiently, her hands folded in her lap. "I have been praying, Charlene, for strength and for God to be ever so near to you and Aimee. I am so sorry," Marcy cried as she embraced Charlene.

Slowly, Marcy guided the vehicle away from the three squished automobiles and into the direction of the hospital. What had exactly happened during the accident was still a mystery yet to be discovered.

As Charlene's mind paddled down the stream of her thoughts, she wondered why God had let this happen. What was the purpose? She already had Todd waiting for her at the lonely, cold hospital, and she definitely did not need Aimee there too. What was happening?

Finally they arrived, and Marcy gently asked, "Would you like us to stay here with you for awhile?" Charlene slowly nodded as tears tinkled from her tired green eyes.

After signing the legal documents for Dr. Jens to operate on Aimee, the three quietly scuttled downstairs to the café. As they slid into a green material booth, Charlene noticed a tear sliding from Jesse's sparkling brown eyes. A long moment of silence followed until Jesse finally forced the words to tumble out of his mouth. Continuously, the tears kept flowing like a thunderous waterfall down his cheek, and as he spoke, he sniffled. "I heard Aimee and her friends planning a drag race at school. As I approached them, an immediate quietness stung the air. Accidentally, I overheard that the race would take place on Maple Avenue this afternoon. I promised myself that I would go down and try to stop them from doing it. I knew God wanted me to. I have been witnessing and praying for them since the beginning of school, and this would be another opportunity. Lives would have been saved if they only had listened. The worst part of it was when Aimee," he paused as if the words stuck to his tongue. Finally, the words poured out like a rushing waterfall thundering into the stream below. "Aimee made fun of God. She completely deteriorated him. I was crushed, completely crushed. How could anyone say something so cruel about God, our Creator who made all things? I just don't understand."

Marcy and Charlene listened attentively as Jesse persisted.

"All seven of them bounded inside the two vehicles, and before I could do anything, they raced down the road. Something inside me knew this wouldn't be good, and as I walked away, I reacted and turned to see the Corvette and the Dodge Charger running a stop sign. They were flying down the road. I would have to say they were going at least 110 km in a fifty zone. It's not like it was a highway. Maple Avenue is a residential area. As they zoomed past the stop sign, a red Explorer collided uncontrollably into the Corvette. Although the Dodge Charger was a few meters behind the Corvette, it was going way too fast to stop. Before I knew it, it had crashed into the red Explorer and the Corvette, causing devastating results. I didn't mean to watch it, but it happened, all in the blink of an eye. The accident oozes back in my mind, and it's horrifying. I feel so awful. I just wish I could have stopped it from happening."

Charlene carried the burden of anxiety. She was worried and fear endlessly gnawed at her soul. Aloud, she uttered, "God is our refuge and strength, a very present help in trouble" (Psalms 46:1, NASB). He will be our comforter. He always is." The pain reflected in her eyes as salty tears flooded down her face. "I am so scared," she cried.

The night continued on. What was going to come of the situation only God knew. As they sat waiting, they decided to pray. Softly, Charlene murmured, "Dear Heavenly Father, I pray that you would protect Aimee and keep her safe. I pray that through this she would come to know you as her personal Savior. We don't understand why this had to happen, and sometimes we aren't meant to. Comfort us and give us strength as we battle this tiresome night ahead. Amen."

Right now, all they could do was wait and pray. Life was turning every which way, and right now, it was on a bumpy bend that led to the unknown. Everything in Charlene's life seemed to be decidedly the worst. God knew the whole plan and the whole outcome. She held onto him as her stronghold even though the fear drained every last bit of strength out of her. God would be her firm foundation to carry her through the terrifying storms in her life. Some that she faced now, while other challenges lay ahead.

Heartbroken

The night dragged on helplessly as Charlene waited in the lonesome waiting room. The small room was filled with scattered chairs along the rusty, majestic walls and in the corner stood a lonely television set. It felt like forever before Tonya, dressed in a straight, white uniform, sauntered toward Charlene. Charlene had arrived at the hospital at four o'clock with Marcy and Jesse, and they had waited with her until eleven o'clock. Now, she was waiting weakly for an update on Aimee. Presently, it was 3:30 a.m., and as tiredness stung her eyelids, she did her best to stay awake. As Tonya staggered toward her, Charlene's mind swirled in circles. Was Aimee going to be all right? Would she make it through this serious accident?

Finally, Tonya whispered, "Mrs. Carter, Aimee is fine. You may go see her if you'd like."

Hastily, Tonya led Charlene to the young girl's room. As Charlene gripped a hold of herself, she nervously strode toward Aimee's bedside. She gasped and clasped one of her hands over her mouth as a tear slipped down her cheek. Aimee looked absolutely awful. The once-beautiful and stunning girl was now terribly bruised.

Ten minutes later, Dr. Jens walked into the dark, quiet room and concisely stated, "Your niece must be very strong. She was the only survivor from the accident, and although she has some major bruises, a few broken ribs, and a broken leg, you should be very thankful. God isn't finished with her yet. She is completely unconscious at the moment, and I anticipate that she will be in a coma for a few days. Keep in mind that time is the key to healing."

"Dr. Jens, were there any difficulties? I have been waiting for over eleven hours," Charlene curiously asked.

Dr. Jens bright expression instantly faded as sadness swept across his face. "Yes, we did experience some problems. Her left leg was completely crushed. We had to operate and realign some of the pieces back together. She would have been paralyzed in that leg if we hadn't. She will need crutches for a few months until her leg has a chance to heal. She'll be fine though, just fine."

"Thank you, Dr. Jens. Thank you," Charlene articulated as he wandered out of the room.

"It is my duty to help those I can. God bless."

Charlene quietly murmured, "Dear God, I thank you. You are so good. You are definitely a miraculous God. Thank you for sparing Aimee's life. I am so grateful. Amen."

Shakily, Charlene sat on the edge of the bed next to Aimee and softly whispered, "Aimee, I love you. I am so sorry for not being the mother you needed. It's just so hard to know how to deal with you sometimes, but I want you to know that it doesn't change the fact that I love you. You are very special to me, and I don't know what I would do without you. You are a daughter to me. You are going to be okay, honey." Quietly, she kissed her forehead, and as tiredness rushed over her, she fell fast asleep in a green, rough chair next to the bed.

The days passed slower than ever. It had been a week from the accident, a tiring and draining week. As Charlene inched her crusty eyes open, she glanced out of the window as the sun shone through, giving the room a sense of hope. Charlene couldn't help but wonder why some people didn't believe there was a God. The flowers were so perfect in their unique own way, and the trees were so bold and strong, their branches stretching over the green, tall grass. Everything had a purpose. Only God could create and align everything so immaculately.

As Charlene turned her attention back to Aimee, she noticed Aimee's eyes flinching open.

"Praise God. Aimee, you are all right," Charlene shouted as she embraced the child.

Aimee managed to find the strength, and in almost a drowned out voice, she gently squeezed her aunt's hand and whispered, "Auntie Charlene, will you forgive me? This time I am not pretending. I understand now, and I want you to know that I love you. You mean so much to me, and I am very thankful you took me into your home. God blessed me with a wonderful mother, and I was so caught up in myself that I didn't realize how blessed I truly am."

Charlene was in complete shock. As the girl glanced at the floor, a tear trickled down her pale cheek. She swallowed hard before continuing, "I remember the day of the accident like it was yesterday. I saw the red vehicle coming, and I screamed. I yelled at Stacie who was beside me to stop. It happened so fast; nothing could be done. Desperately, I called out to your God, and I promised him I would change if he were truly real. As the vehicles collided, I saw a white angelic figure walking toward me, and I thought I was imagining. He said, 'I am the Way, and the Truth, and the Life; no one comes to the Father but through Me' (John 14:6, NASB). He then reached out his hand to me, and I took a hold of it. Auntie, it was Jesus. It was like a peace renewed my soul, and for some strange reason, I knew I would be okay."

It was a marveling story, God's miraculous plan to completely change the life of a rebellious girl and call her his child.

"God, thank you for giving Aimee a second chance to live, an opportunity to live for you. Walk with her in all she does. Amen," Charlene exclaimed.

A moment later, Aimee gently asked, "Auntie, how do I give my life over to Christ? I know he is real. He saved my life. I love him more than anything I have ever loved before. He is everything to me," Aimee paused as a tear slid from beneath the corner of her eye. Charlene could see the pain and guilt reflecting in the girl's baby-blue eyes as Aimee let the tears drain from within. "I feel so awful. I kept telling Jesse that God wasn't real. I mocked God. I didn't believe because he took away everything I have ever loved. But now I know God is real. I believe by faith that he is. I just don't know how God will ever forgive me for what I have done. I just feel this guilt seizing every area of my soul."

"God is able to forgive you, Aimee. Jesus died for our sins, so God could forgive us, and so we could be saved. You just have to tell him. He knows your heart."

Slowly, Aimee began, "Dear Heavenly Father, please forgive me for all my sins. Forgive me for rejecting and mocking you. I feel absolutely terrible. Cleanse me and make me pure in your sight. Please come and reign in my life. I am nothing without you. I believe that Jesus died on the cross and paid for my sins, so I could be saved. I believe that Jesus rose again. Fill my life, God. I want with my whole heart to follow you. Amen."

After witnessing the joyful, life-changing event, Charlene wiped the continuous tears from her green eyes. It was a turning point in the young girl's life. Charlene saw a yearning, a sudden change in Aimee's life to live for Christ. Why did God give Aimee another chance? It was because he gave everyone a second chance. He had a plan for her life, a reason she survived the traumatizing event. God had given Aimee opportunities to come and follow him, but when she kept rejecting him, drastic measures occurred. It was the only way to get her attention. Charlene had never imagined that this day would ever come or if it did, it would come much later in Aimee's life. Charlene was so excited. God had answered her prayer. It truly was a celebration.

Finally after another long week, Aimee was released from the hospital's care and was able to go home. Dr. Jens had strongly advised Charlene to homeschool Aimee for the rest of the year. It would be hard on Aimee to answer all the questions the other students had regarding the accident. Besides, Aimee had already missed two weeks, and she was behind all the other kids. At this point, homeschooling was definitely a better option.

As Charlene pulled out the keys from the ignition, she opened the car door and walked around to the other side. Helping Aimee out of the Durango, Charlene guided her up the cement walkway towards the antique home. She unlocked the front door, and Aimee braced herself against her crutches as she slowly made her way to the soft, black leather couch in the living room.

As she rested her body against the cool leather, she sweetly asked, "Auntie Charlene, I was wondering if you had an extra Bible that I could have. I am really eager to read God's Word, his gift to us."

"Of course, Aimee. I will go and get one," Charlene replied as she scuttled to her bedroom to retrieve a Bible.

After finding a brown leather Bible, Charlene presented it to the young girl. "Here you go, sweetie. My parents bought this Bible for me on my sixteenth birthday, and now I want you to have it." Charlene looked off into the distance as her mind traveled the road back to her past. "It seems like just yesterday when I was your age. You have so much life left to live, and I want you to know that having God as your main priority truly is the best thing in this world. I have been a Christian since I was a young girl, but I never understood that God needed to be my main priority, the only one I live for. Only this past year did I realize it, and I see life from a different perspective now. Life is worth living. My sister once told me that without God there is no hope, no reason to live. God is our hope, the only reason to live. In Christ, you are made truly alive. It is a very true statement."

"I will treasure this Bible always. Thank you, Mom," Aimee blurted, and as an embarrassing, pale expression flooded her face, she quickly corrected herself. "Auntie. Thank you, Auntie."

As Charlene waltzed into the bright, yellow kitchen to prepare supper, she noticed the answering machine light flashing, indicating there was a missed call. Rapidly, she pushed the button, and to her surprise, a strange man's voice boomed through the room. "Hello, Aimee, this is Mr. Murphy. I am very disappointed in you since you were supposed to be here an hour ago. I was counting on you being here, and I told Billy he could have today off. I thought we agreed on you working this afternoon. Anyways, there is nothing that can be done about it now. Give me a call as soon as you receive this message. Thanks. Bye."

"I completely forgot. That must have been weeks ago that he called. With the accident and all, I just couldn't have remembered to phone him. Mr. Murphy sure is going to be mad," Charlene said, as though she were about to cry. Everything inside her crashed, and as she slid to the floor, the tears and agony streamed out of her. "Todd, where is my Todd? What is happening to me? I am falling a part."

Charlene recovered herself and slowly stood up. "Aimee, could you call Mr. Murphy and tell him what is going on. I just need to be alone for a moment." She breathed deeply and ambled into her bedroom. As she lowered herself onto the bed, she reached for her Bible that was lying on the nightstand. Quickly, she flipped the thick pages until she found a certain portion of Scripture and read it aloud.

> When you pray, you are not to be like the hypocrites; for they love to stand and pray in the synagogues and on the street corners so that they may be seen by men. Truly I say to you, they have their reward in full. But you, when you pray, go into your inner room, close your door and pray to your Father who is in secret, and your Father who sees what is done in secret will reward you.

> And when you are praying, do not use meaningless repetition as the Gentiles do, for they suppose that they will be heard for their many words. So do not be like them; for your Father knows what you need before you ask Him.
>
> Pray, then, in this way: "Our Father who is in heaven, hallowed be Your name. Your kingdom come. Your will be done, on earth as it is in heaven. Give us this day our daily bread. And forgive us our debts, as we also have forgiven our debtors. And do not lead us into temptation, but deliver us from evil. For Yours is the kingdom and the power and the glory forever. Amen."
>
> For if you forgive others for their transgressions, your heavenly Father will also forgive you. But if you do not forgive others, then your Father will not forgive your transgressions.
>
> Matthew 6:5–15 (NASB)

Quietly, she placed her Bible on the nightstand and softly whispered, "'Our Father who is in heaven, hallowed be your name. Your kingdom come. Your will be done, on earth as it is in heaven. Give us this day our daily bread. And forgive us our debts as we also have forgiven our debtors. And do not lead us into temptation, but deliver us from evil. For yours is the kingdom and the power and the glory forever. Amen.'"

She gradually arose and a peace flooded inside her. It was a peace from God. The peace he had always promised.

Slowly, she strode back to the kitchen. "Aimee, did you call Mr. Murphy?"

"Yes, I did. I told him I would come in this weekend. He said he wishes me all the best. He also said he was sorry for sounding so gruff on the phone. He felt bad because he didn't know I was in a car accident," Aimee sweetly said before burying her head back into the Bible.

Charlene instantly began peeling potatoes, and she couldn't help but notice Aimee so intrigued by God's Word. Aimee truly had changed. A desire to change and explore God's Word replaced the self-centered attitude that once had occupied the young, spirited girl. It lit a flame of hope for Aimee that there was a reason to live, to live for Jesus Christ. It was a true and dedicated change from her heart, not a superficial change to make her look good on the outside. She yearned wholeheartedly for God to fill her up with his undivided love and to build a strong relationship with him.

"Auntie Charlene, I have a question. I am reading the book of Genesis. Do you think that God loved Adam and Eve as much as he did even after they sinned?" The confusion mirrored in the girl's eyes.

"Aimee, there was no sin before Adam and Eve disobeyed God, right? Well, it was the fall of man. It wasn't that God didn't love them anymore because he did. He loved us so much that he sent his Son to die on the cross for our sins, so we could be made in right relationship to God. 'But God demonstrates His own love toward us, in that while we were yet sinners, Christ died for us' [Romans 5:8, NASB]. It also says in a later part of Romans, 'But in all these things we overwhelmingly conquer through Him who loved us. For I am convinced that neither death, nor life, nor angels, nor principalities, nor things present, nor things to come, nor powers, nor height, nor depth, nor any other created thing, will be able to separate us from the love of God, which is in Christ Jesus our Lord' [Romans 8:37–38, NASB]. God loves everyone. he doesn't love our sin, but it will never change how much he loves us. God is not proud when we do wrong; it makes him sad, but he never stops loving us. God loves you, Aimee, and he has forgiven you. But we need to understand that we can't just do whatever we want and then ask for forgiveness. We need to live for Christ. Truly in our hearts, we have to be sorry, repent, and ask for forgiveness. God can only forgive when we ask him to, and there must be an evident change in our lives."

"I am so happy and overflowed with joy. I just can't express how God has changed my life; he just has. The half that was missing in my life is now completely whole. God is the only one that can make people happy. No matter what one has, even if it is absolutely everything one could dream of, God is the only one who can make us truly glad inside. He is worth living for. I think a lot of people don't realize that God is everything we need. We try and look elsewhere for happiness, but we can never find it." A grin stretched across Aimee's sweet, tiny face. "God has made my life worth the living."

"That is the way God intended it to be. He loves when we love him."

As Charlene continued peeling potatoes and placing them in a huge pot full of water, she took notice of Aimee folding her hands and softly praying, loud enough for Charlene to interpret what she was saying.

"Dear God, please forgive me for being so wrong and disobeying the leadership and authority you set before me. Auntie Charlene was only setting boundaries for my own good, so I would not encounter situations that would lead to destruction. God, I wish I could change my past, all that I have done. If only I could go back in time to the afternoon of the drag race. I would stand firm beside Jesse and would not waver from you. I would try to stop the illegal act from happening. If I only had stood up for what was right, nine people would have been alive today. It's my fault, and I know I will have to live with the guilt and reminder of taking part in killing those people. Forevermore, I promise I will stand up for you because you have given me hope and a reason to live. I realize how wrong I was, and I pray you will heal the wounds my sins have caused. I thank you for giving me a second chance to live, to live for you, God. I am very grateful to you for transforming my life. Before I was such a mess and completely confused. With your strength, give me the courage to face each new day. In Christ's name, I pray. Amen."

A gentle smile formed across Charlene's face, and in her heart, she truly believed that Aimee had changed. Time would be the key to what next exciting or traumatic event would take another piece in the mysterious puzzle of life.

Days of Healing

June announced its beginning, and the sun shone forth its warm glow over the earth. It had been difficult adjusting to everything that had happened, but somehow Charlene seemed to manage. Aimee was slowly recovering from her injuries; it would take time to restore her strength. Gradually, she reinforced her ability to walk, but she still used the support of her crutches to move around.

Dr. Jens suggestion of homeschooling had been the perfect answer to Charlene's dilemma. Since Aimee was still too weak to return to school, Charlene had deemed it appropriate to let the girl rest and recuperate while still staying on top of her homework at home.

It was a warm summer Friday, and the flowers revealed God's beautiful creation as the buds were rich in bloom. Suddenly, the doorbell chimed, and Charlene instantly scurried to retrieve it. To her surprise, there in the doorway stood a handsome young man.

"Hello, Jesse. Aimee is in the living room finishing up her school for the weekend. You can come in."

"Thank you, Mrs. Carter. I'll only be staying for a few minutes. I have to help my dad at the farm for the rest of the afternoon."

Slowly, he strode towards the black couch where Aimee sat occupied by her work.

"Hi, Aimee. Is your leg feeling any better today? I miss you," Jesse proudly announced as he gently handed her a bouquet of beautiful scented tiger lilies. Staring into his dark-brown eyes, Aimee softly smiled, and for a moment, they locked gazes. Slowly, he leaned down and tenderly kissed her forehead. "I should go now. I just wanted to see how you were doing."

"Thank you for the flowers. It was very thoughtful of you."

As he escorted himself to the front door, he abruptly turned around and grinned. "You're welcome. I am happy to do it. Oh, and by the way, I was wondering if you wanted to go for a walk later. I know you are still using your crutches, but I thought we could take it slow. Might be good for you."

"I need some fresh air anyways. I would love that."

"I'll come here after I finish helping my dad with some of the farm chores. It will probably be in about an hour and a half."

"All right. I'll see you later," Aimee hollered as Jesse closed the door behind him.

Instantly, Charlene waltzed into the living room and pronounced, "I am going to visit Todd for half an hour. Are you going to be all right by yourself?"

"Of course, Auntie. I am just starting Exodus in the Bible. It is actually very interesting. I'll be fine, and I won't cause any trouble. I promise."

"I know, Aimee. I trust you. I know that you truly have changed. Bye."

Quickly, Charlene fumbled for her car keys that were hiding inside her purse and strutted out the door.

Upon arriving at the hospital, Charlene swiftly sauntered upstairs to Todd's lonely hospital room.

"Hi, Todd. I love you, darling. I am so happy to be here with you." Suddenly everything she held inside her shattered. Would Todd ever wake up from a coma? In some cases, it took twenty years. She was becoming restless waiting, but she never lost faith that God could perform a miracle. He was truly a miraculous God. He had the plan all sorted out; there was no need to worry.

Hesitantly, she sat down in her usual chair that was next to Todd's bed and firmly gripped his sturdy hand in her own. "You are going to be okay. Deep inside my heart I know that you will wake up. It will just be in God's perfect timing not mine. Hold on, darling."

For a short half hour, Charlene talked to Todd and told him all about the drastic change that took place in Aimee's life. "You would be so proud. You have a beautiful niece who has grown into our daughter. She is an amazing girl, you know." She then smiled as she placed his rough hand on her round stomach. "This is your baby, Todd. I'm due in a month's time so please come home to me. I need you."

Finally, she arose and rubbed Todd's brow. "I have to go now, Todd, but I will see you soon. I love you."

As Charlene departed, she maneuvered her Durango into the clear direction of home. It was going to be a gorgeous evening. The cloudless sky was warm and welcoming.

Slowly, Charlene parked her vehicle on the driveway and hurried up the walkway to the front door. Fidgeting to twist the knob, Charlene finally opened it and was greeted by the cool air flooding from inside.

"Aimee, have you eaten supper yet? Since tomorrow is Saturday, I thought we could watch a movie."

"No, I haven't had dinner yet. I am so captivated by the book of Exodus, and I just couldn't put it down. Oh, I forgot to ask you if it was okay if I went for a walk with Jesse in about forty-five minutes. A movie night would have been lots of fun though."

"That is completely fine, Aimee. I hope you have a wonderful time."

Suddenly, the doorbell buzzed, and Charlene quickly answered it.

"Mom and Dad. What are you doing here?" Charlene's face revealed her astonishment.

"You know how much we love surprises." Her dad laughed as he embraced his stunned daughter. Her father was an elderly man with pure white hair. His tangled beard was a cloudy gray, and his eyes were a soft hazelnut-brown. His slender frame stretched to almost six feet.

"Well, come on in and make yourselves comfortable. I would like you to meet—" Charlene began, but before she could finish, her mother rapidly interrupted her.

"Oh, did the baby arrive early? Why didn't you tell us? Is it a boy or a girl? Where is my grandbaby?" her mother asked in a slightly frazzled tone.

"Mom, can't you see that the baby is still in here?" Charlene tried not to giggle as she placed a warm hand on her bulging stomach.

"Oh, dear me. Forgive me, Charlene. Now, who is it then that you want us to meet?" Her mother's face instantaneously flushed an embarrassing pale color.

Charlene swiftly sauntered into the living room and helped Aimee balance on her crutches. As she guided Aimee to the entryway, Charlene's mother's mouth dropped wide open.

"This is Aimee, my niece. A few months after her mother died the Children's Aid Foundation contacted me and asked if I would be willing to take her in. She is a new and wonderful addition to our family."

Aimee cheerfully smiled as she politely said, "Hello. Is it okay if I call you my grandparents? I have never really had any before."

"Of course, child. We would love to have another granddaughter," Charlene's father kindly uttered.

Suddenly, Charlene's mother inspected the girl over carefully. "What in the world happened to you, dear?"

Charlene directed everyone to the bright, yellow kitchen as Aimee proceeded to answer her grandmother's abrupt concern.

"A few months ago I came to live here, even though I did not really want to. Purposefully, I did everything against my aunt Charlene's counsel. After I was involved in a serious car accident, I saw my life flash before my very eyes. I knew in my heart that the only reason worth living was for the Lord. I accepted Christ as my personal Savior while I was in the hospital, and ever since that day, a beautiful journey began—my walk with Christ. A special verse I hold dear to my heart is 'I am the Way, and the Truth, and the Life; no one comes to the Father but through Me' (John 14:6, NASB)."

Suddenly, the sweet, rich sound of a bell chimed, and Charlene strutted towards the door. As she screeched the beautiful stained antique door open, she joyously exclaimed, "Good evening, Jesse. Aimee told me you two were going for a stroll in the park nearby. I will go and get her. Aimee!"

As Aimee wobbled to the door, a bright, cheery grin swept across Jesse's face. "Hello, Aimee. It is good to see you walking on two feet. Where are your crutches? I thought you needed them."

"I do, but my aunt put them in the closet."

"Oh, let me get them for you." Jesse quickly opened the closet door in the front entry where many jackets had found a cozy home. When he handed her the crutches, their eyes locked in an intense gaze. It was a romantic, sweet moment Aimee would never forget.

Slowly, they made their way out of the house and towards the park nearby.

The summer evening breeze outside was warm and brisk as it scattered Aimee's long blond hair across her face. They walked unhurriedly, so Aimee could brace herself with her crutches at a comfortable, easy going pace. It was so good to be outside in the fresh air; the majestic scenery splashed a warm sensation in Aimee's heart. The daisies were bountiful in fragrance, and the night was delicate. It was absolutely gorgeous.

Jesse and Aimee strolled quietly until finally he broke the warm, inviting silence. "I have been trying to find the courage to ask you if you would come to youth with me tonight at my church? I know your grandparents are here and all, but I thought I'd ask anyways."

A soft, gentle smile formed daintily across Aimee's face as she stared into his fierce chocolate-brown eyes. "I would love to come if it is all right with my Auntie. I'll ask her when we get back to my house."

Something inside her made her heart soar abstractedly with wild dreams. Perhaps Jesse was the man God had for her. She supposed only time would tell.

Whispering a sweet, melodic song, the wind whisked the thin branches of the trees as they ambled along.

Finally, it was Aimee's turn to find strength. "Jesse, do you really think that God loves me as much as he loves people who haven't made the same mistakes I have? I know that God has forgiven me for my sins, but it just seems as though he shouldn't love me as much as, take yourself for instance."

"Hold on, Aimee. I may not have made the same decisions you have, but I am not perfect either. I have made many mistakes in my life that I regret. We are all sinners, and God loves us all the same, no more, no less. We are all equally loved by God."

Blinking back the immediate swarm of tears, Aimee tried to hold them in, but they hurriedly escaped out of the corner of her eyes. Slowly, Jesse grabbed her hand and gripped it firmly in his.

"Do you want to sit down for a few minutes? It is going to be okay." Jesse embraced her for a moment as she let the tears soak into his navy T-shirt.

Finally, she glanced up into his eyes and smiled. "I have never met anyone like you, Jesse. You are a rare and precious gem. You really are special to me."

"And, Aimee, you have no idea how much you mean to me. I knew I could never date you because you weren't a Christian. 'Do not be bound together with unbelievers; for what partnership have righteousness and lawlessness, or what fellowship has light with darkness' (2 Corinthians 6:14, NASB). When I found out that you gave your life over to the Lord, I was so excited. Not just because I could possibly date you in the future but moreover because God became a part of your life. I can tell that you have changed; you're different, a good different. It is absolutely awesome, and I just can't describe how happy I am for you."

"Jesse, I wanted to apologize for the things I said the day of the accident. I feel so awful. I always knew in my heart that I was missing something, but I didn't really want to find it. I guess I was just so confused to who I was or who I wanted to be. I am just so thankful that God chose me to be his child. It is truly exciting."

"Aimee, you are so precious to me, and no words can even describe how I feel about you. You are a princess of the King, God our Heavenly Father."

As they sat on the wooden park bench, Jesse attempted to explain the answer to Aimee's troubling question. It was a question she had pondered for many days, a question beyond her understanding.

"Aimee, you have to put the past behind you and move on. God loves you just as much as anyone and has forgiven you completely by his grace. He died on the cross for you and for me, for every single person so we could be saved. When Jesus was crucified, there were two thieves hung on either side of him." Jesse paused as he quickly grabbed a tiny, white Bible from his back pocket.

> Now there was also an inscription above Him, "THIS IS THE KING OF THE JEWS." One of the criminals who were hanged there was hurling abuse at Him, saying, "Are You not the Christ? Save Yourself and us!" But the other answered, and rebuking him said, "Do you not even fear God, since you are under the same sentence of condemnation? And we indeed are suffering justly, for we are receiving what we deserve for our deeds; but this man has

> done nothing wrong." And he was saying, "Jesus, remember me when You come in Your kingdom!" And He said to him, "Truly I say to you, today you shall be with Me in Paradise."
>
> Luke 23:38–43 (NASB)

"Aimee, he was a robber, and God loved him so much. The man confessed that he had done something worth dying for, and he knew in his heart that Jesus was the Son of God. Jesus didn't say that because the man had stolen he would never see his kingdom. Rather Jesus extended grace to the man, breathing life into his very soul. Whatever your past is, God has forgiven it. Aimee, God loves you more than the entire universe itself."

Gently, Jesse placed his hand on her face and wiped a runaway tear that escaped down her cheek. A faint smile sweetly crawled upon her face.

After they rose to their feet, Jesse grasped her hand as they walked home. Finally, after arriving at the rustic abode, Jesse guided her up the front concrete steps.

"I will phone you once I ask my aunt if I can come to youth tonight. When does it start? It is only five right now," Aimee sweetly articulated.

"It starts at eight. I really hope that you can come." He smiled as he strutted to his old truck that was parked on the driveway. Slowly, she unlocked the door and stepped inside the cool house. The rush of cold air felt so good and refreshing.

"Hello, is anybody here? I am home," Aimee called out. The quiet house swirled with emptiness as if it were an abandoned ghost town. Where had everyone gone? A half hour ago everyone was there. The mystery agonized her to no end as the tenseness crept up and overwhelmed her. As she calmed down, she hurriedly picked up a note that had fallen on the floor in the kitchen. It read:

Aimee,

Emergency! We will be back in a while.
Don't worry.
Help yourself to some food in the fridge
just in case we are not home for supper.
Love you lots, and we will see you hope-
fully soon.
#403-527-4037

Love,
Auntie Charlene

What in the world was going on?

Pray for a Miracle

Frantically, Aimee snatched the black phone off the yellow wall and rapidly punched in her aunt's cell phone number. Upon receiving the answering machine, Aimee spoke with sheer confidence, hiding the fact that she was terribly frightened. "Hi, Auntie Charlene, this is Aimee. I just discovered your note. If you could call me back and let me know what is going on, that would be fantastic. Thanks. Bye." Everything inside her collapsed instantaneously. What should she do?

The hospital had a lonely, cold, tense feeling. The beautiful sun barely shone through the drapery on the windows. As Charlene and her parents followed Dr. Jens up to Todd's room, Charlene's heart pounded fiercely. What had happened to Todd? She prayed wholeheartedly that he was all right. He just had to be.

"I am afraid that your husband is dead," Dr. Jens began as they entered the small room.

What? Had Charlene heard right? Todd was dead? Her heart immediately stopped pounding as the endless tears came. Todd couldn't be dead, he just couldn't be. Dr. Jens abrupt and terrifying news created a bubbling volcano that erupted inside Charlene. She had lost Nate and now, she had lost Todd too. Every man she had ever loved was taken away from her. What was going on?

"God, be with me, please. I can't stand to hear the rest. Don't leave me; don't leave. 'God is our refuge and strength, a very present help in trouble' (Psalms 46:1 NASB). Help me, God, please," Charlene murmured under her breath.

As Dr. Jens continued, she felt like fainting. "Well, actually, he isn't quite dead, but he is close enough that I can almost promise you he is not ever going to wake up from his state of a coma. I hope you understand how serious his accident was. I would personally advise you to let us give him a good death. Euthanasia is the best option you have. If I were you, I would most definitely choose this procedure. It's the only choice you have."

Charlene screamed with terror. She would never allow Dr. Jens to perform euthanasia to her Todd, ever. She would not purposely kill Todd. God performed miracles, and she believed that whether or not Todd woke up was completely up to God. Whatever purpose God had for Todd's accident would go, and Charlene would not interfere in any way.

"That's murder! You are killing an innocent life. How could you even suggest it? I have other options, and killing Todd is not one of them. God is a miraculous God, and for some reason Todd hasn't died yet. It is in God's hands, not mine."

She needed Todd there with her as long as God wanted him to be. Hope was what she needed. And God was her hope. He had been there for her, and he would never leave. He was truly everything she needed.

"Would you like to think about it for a while, maybe a night to sleep on it?" Dr. Jens asked.

Panting for small breaths of air, Charlene calmly blurted, "No, and I won't tell you again. No further procedures for killing my husband will be necessary. I have already stated my reasons."

"Mrs. Carter, I don't think you understand how serious your husband's situation is. He is nearly dead. You are just prolonging his death."

The firm glare clarified her position on the matter, and Dr. Jens briefly stated, "All right, no further procedures will be done. Good day, Mrs. Carter."

Charlene's thoughts continued to spin inside her head until finally she collapsed. Thankfully, Todd wasn't dead. A small weight had been lifted off her as everything that had taken place registered in her mind.

As the three slowly trudged to the parking lot, the tears blazed from her stiff and tired eyes. Climbing into her parents' vehicle, Charlene sat in the back, letting the strained tears run wild and free.

Hurt and pain overflowed in Charlene's heart. She was having a hard-enough time with Todd being in a coma, but Todd being gone forever was too much for her to handle. She had already lost Nate. She couldn't bear to lose Todd too. Todd was still alive, and there was still hope. If Dr. Jens proceeded to do euthanasia to him, he would never see their dear, beloved baby. She had to have faith that in God's time he would bring him through.

As Charlene's father parked the vehicle in front of the antique home, Charlene wiped the damp tears from her face with the back of her hand. Swiftly, she crawled from the backseat and marched up the cement walkway. As she inched the front door open, Aimee wobbled to the entry to meet them.

Swallowing hard to fight back the worried tears, Aimee clearly asked, "What's going on? It's Uncle Todd, isn't it?"

Quivering helplessly, Charlene stared into space as if everything in the world had suddenly stopped. She was as dead inside as a lifeless creature. As she embraced the child, she quietly muttered, forcing the mumbled words out, "Uncle Todd is not doing well at all. Dr. Jens said he doesn't have a chance of surviving. He said Todd is almost dead."

As Aimee tried to comfort her aunt, a quiet, gentle tear trickled in a curved, rocky path down Charlene's cheek. Aimee could not stand to see her aunt in so much agonizing pain. Her aunt had done so much for her, and Aimee thought of her as her own mother. God knew how much she needed a loving mother, and for whatever reason, God had chosen Charlene to fulfill that need.

As they sat around the kitchen table for supper, the phone continuously rang. Finally, Aimee limped to retrieve it.

"Hello. I'm not sure if I can go tonight. Well, there has just been a lot going on. All right, bye."

Sitting back down at the table, Aimee gracefully grabbed a chocolate chip cookie.

A questioned look seeped onto Charlene's serene face. "Not going where? Were you planning on going somewhere with Jesse this evening?"

Shyly, Aimee responded, "Jesse asked me if I wanted to go to youth with him at his church tonight, but with all that has happened to Uncle Todd, I decided to stay here for the evening."

Smiling softly, Charlene glanced at the hardware floor. "Aimee, no, you should go. Uncle Todd is just fine. He'll be okay." She squeezed back the tears. In all honesty, she didn't know if Todd was going to be okay. She just didn't know.

"Thank you, Auntie Charlene. I'll quickly phone Jesse back and let him know." Swiftly, Aimee grabbed the black smooth phone and dialed the Stanford's number.

"Hello. This is Aimee."

"Hi, Aimee. It's Karla. Jesse is outside right now feeding the horses."

"I just wanted to tell him that I am going to come to youth tonight. My aunt said that it would be just fine."

"I'll tell him. He will be so excited. You have no idea how much he talks about you. Anyways, my mom wanted to offer to pick you up. Jesse told us that your grandparents are visiting."

"Thank you. I would really appreciate that. See you tonight, Karla."

"All right. We'll probably be there in about half an hour. Bye."

After Aimee clicked the telephone into its rightful home, she hurriedly scrambled to her bedroom. She brushed her long, shiny blond hair and rapidly fixed her dainty makeup.

Finally, the crisp ring of a doorbell echoed through the house, and Charlene scurried to the front. "Hi, Marcy. It is so good to see you."

"You too, Charlene. Here, I wanted you to know that our family is thinking and praying for you."

Gratefully, Charlene accepted the small gift.

"I will bring Aimee home at around ten. Take care, my friend," Marcy uttered as she quickly hugged Charlene.

Aimee braced herself as she clung tightly to her metal crutches. Without hesitation, Jesse offered his assistance by helping her inside the mini van where Karla sat impatiently. Taking her crutches, he carefully slipped them in the small trunk in the back.

As the white vehicle compelled down the smooth, paved street, Charlene slowly unwrapped the thoughtful present. In her tiny hands, she cradled a wooden angel. An engraving was carved on the bottom of the figurine's dress, "I can do all things through Christ who gives me strength" (Philippians 4:13, NIV). It was a strong encouragement to her at this time, and it was exactly what she needed to hear. It gave her hope to keep persevering.

Gently, she positioned the angelic figure on the wooden coffee table in the living room. That way she could look at the verse every day and be reminded of God's promise.

At the youth Bible study, Jesse introduced Aimee to two Christian girls sitting with his sister, Karla, on a dark-brown leather sofa in the corner.

"This is Brandy, Tiffany, and my sister, Karla, who you kind of already know," Jesse declared.

Brandy had long light-brown hair and twinkling ocean-blue eyes. Accompanying her was a sweet and shy personality.

Perky Tiffany was tall and petite and wavy dark-blond hair outlined her soft, small face. Her outgoing livelihood created a sense of maturity.

Jesse's younger sister Karla had a heart of an angel. Her outward appearance showed off her natural curly reddish-blond hair and her stunning green eyes.

Aimee knew in her heart that these girls could become true and loyal friends who would stand beside her and be a living testimony to encourage her in her walk with God. It was such a blessing. God had provided for her just as he had promised.

During the Bible study, the youth pastor Tom, talked about the issues that teenagers of today face. On a big, white dry-erase board, Tom scribbled the words drugs, alcohol, smoking, and gossip. After elaborating on each topic, Tom shared some of the struggles in his life that he had been challenged with. When he told the youth a story about his past, he described the details of his position and how he felt.

"I wanted to be accepted, to have friends. Little did I know that they weren't really my friends. To be accepted, I felt the need to step out of the parental boundaries my parents had set for the sake of own good. I felt lonely like nobody cared. My past is full of many regrets I wish I could change. But it all comes down to this, I can't. Almost all of these categories can fall under peer pressure. To fit in you have to do this and you have to be that. They are all lies, and we believe them. To be honest, I believed them.

"It was my sophomore year when I became grossly involved with drugs, alcohol, and cigarettes. It was the popular thing to do, and I wanted so desperately to fit in. As a result, I gave into peer pressure that was knocking at my door. I didn't stand against it like I should have. I welcomed it into my life. When all the guys went drinking, I went too. Whatever people of this world did, I did. But God says do not be of this world." Pastor Tom reached for his Bible and quickly flipped the thin pages to a specific scripture. "John writes, 'Do not love the world nor the things in the world. If anyone loves the world, the love of the Father is not in him. For all that is in the world, the lust of the flesh and the lust of the eyes and the boastful pride of life, is not from the Father, but is from the world. The world is passing away, and also its lusts; but the one who does the will of God lives forever' [1 John 2:15–17, NASB].

"God wants us to get rid of our old self, our old sinful ways, and live a life that is pleasing to him. Don't give into peer pressure. You will always have regrets when you do, always. Jesus is the way, the only way to the Father."

Pastor Tom then asked if anyone would like to share anything that related to any of the topics. Feeling God gently tug on her heart, Aimee bravely spoke with clear confidence, "Several months ago, my mother died, and I was sent to the Children's Aid Foundation, which is an orphanage. After the foundation contacted my aunt, I came to live with her. I knew a little about God. When I was a young girl, my uncle Todd took me to church, and I was so eager to learn about him. However, I never accepted Christ as my Savior because once my dad died I didn't think I had any reason to. I blamed God for my father's death, and when my mom passed away too, it further justified my initial argument for not believing. I couldn't help but wonder what kind of a God would just let my whole family die and leave me here alone. That was when I completely shut myself off from God.

"Recently, I was involved in a drag race, which resulted in a serious accident. As you can tell, I crushed my leg. As the vehicles collided, I saw Jesus. He said, 'I am the Way, and the Truth, and the Life; no one comes to the Father but through Me' [John 14:6, NASB]. God gave me a second chance, and I realized that it wasn't God's fault my parents died. I accepted Jesus as my personal Savior, and I am on such a beautiful journey, a journey that has changed my life. It is absolutely amazing. The choices I made then still affect my life, but I thank God everyday for the second chance to live a life that is pleasing to him. I can't change my past, and I wish I could because—" The tears unknowingly slipped down the side of her cheeks, and as she proceeded, her voice became slightly shaky. "I was a part of killing eight other lives. My close friend begged us to stop, but I ignored his advice. What I am saying is that peer pressure and all the other related subjects didn't get me anywhere. God truly is the only one who satisfies."

Although Aimee had not known it at the time, she had just given her testimony to over thirty kids. She was already a shining light for Christ.

"Thank you, Aimee. Wow, that is an amazing testimony. Thanks for sharing. To wrap it up, I just want to say we all have something about our past that haunts us. We are all sinners, and we all have regrets. However, God doesn't want us to look to the right or to the left or behind us, but He wants us to look straight ahead at Jesus Christ. We need to leave our past behind and our worries to the side. We need to be of Christ and let his light so shine. We need to make a difference. Let's pray."

After the final closing prayer, Cara passed a dish full of homemade chocolate peanut butter squares around the large circle. The sweet, fresh aroma filled the room as they all ate the scrumptious dessert. It was a wonderful evening, and at nine thirty, Aimee quickly said good-bye to Brandy and Tiffany as Marcy graciously waited to drive her home.

"Thank you so much, Mrs. Stanford. Bye Jesse and Karla. That was so much fun. I would most definitely go again," Aimee politely verbalized as Marcy rolled to a complete stop in front of her aunt's house.

After Aimee was inside the air-conditioned abode, she quickly scampered to the bathroom to brush her teeth and to slip into her pajamas. As she snuggled under her cozy, turquoise and brown comforter, she sincerely whispered a prayer from her heart, "Thank you, God, for such an amazing evening and for blessing me with a few strong Christian friends. I also want to thank you for loving me as much as you love everyone else despite my inadequacies. I want to use this second chance you have graciously given to me to be a living testimony for you. Thank you for Jesse. He really is a fantastic guy who has a strong relationship with you. God, you are his first priority, and I want more than anything for you to be mine. God, please also be with Uncle Todd. If it is your will, perform a miracle. I love you so much. Thanks for everything. Amen."

After finishing her short heartfelt prayer, she fell into a deep sleep. It had been a marvelous night to learn and grow in her knowledge and understanding of who God was. It had also been a blessing for her to be able to share her testimony. Every day she felt closer and closer to God, her Heavenly Father. In everything, she just wanted to live a life that was pleasing to him.

Time of Sorrow

The days quickly passed, and the bright, sizzling sun scorched its hot rays over the earth as summer swirled around in the air. The dark, healthy, green grass carpeted the ground in front of Charlene's house as the July wind twirled the sweet pink blossoms here and there.

After a few short weeks, Charlene's parents departed from Edmonton and went back to South Carolina. As she waved farewell, a sudden, sharp pain tore at her lower abdomen. Slowly, she lowered herself down onto the grass to catch her breath. It was almost as if the wind was knocked right out of her. Clutching the sod to relieve some of the pain, Charlene scrunched up her face in anguish. The sharpness stung continuously, and she feared it would never let go.

"I have to phone Dr. Stella right away. Ugh!" Charlene screamed in agony. As she rose, she planted her feet on the grass and awkwardly toddled inside the house.

"God, be with me. I feel like I am going to die. Amen," Charlene whispered as she staggered to the phone. The sweat dripped from her brow as she dialed the number.

"Hello, this is Dr. Stella's office. How can I help you?" the receptionist politely asked.

"My name is Charlene Carter. I am having a piercing pain in my lower abdomen. I would like to book an appointment to see Dr. Stella as soon as possible," Charlene stuttered.

"There is an opening in three days, this coming Wednesday at two o'clock in the afternoon. Does that work for you?"

"Yes, thank you. I'll see you then. Bye." Charlene clicked the phone into its holder and stumbled to the black leather couch in the living room.

"Aimee, I need some water," Charlene hollered as she stretched her aching body onto the comfortable sofa. Her mind was spinning rapidly, and when Aimee did not respond, everything suddenly triggered. Her parents had taken Aimee to the Murphy's general store on their way out of town.

Charlene gently closed her tired eyes and drifted off into a dreamy sleep. If she were asleep, she wouldn't feel this traumatizing, continuous pain. Everything would be just fine or at least she hoped it would.

At four o'clock in the late afternoon, Charlene opened her stiff eyes. Everything seemed to be a daze. The entire room was blurry and foggy and was spinning around her. A soft, gentle voice whispered to her, but she couldn't register what the person was saying. When Charlene realized what was going on, she snapped out of it.

"Auntie Charlene, are you all right? I have been trying to talk to you for the past twenty minutes. You wouldn't wake up. You look really pale," Aimee worriedly said.

"I am completely fine, really. It's nothing at all." Charlene forced herself to be brave.

"I think I should take you to the hospital. Something is terribly wrong."

"No, I will be as good as new in the morning. I think I will just go to bed right now. I am just overtired," Charlene whispered as she stood up.

Swiftly, Charlene bustled to her bedroom and climbed inside the cool covers. As she shut her eyes, she instantaneously fell asleep.

Finally, Wednesday arrived, and Charlene hurried to the hospital for her appointment. She seemed to feel worse and worse as each day passed. Hopefully, Dr. Stella would be able to confirm what was going on.

As she slowly trudged into the waiting room, she quietly sat in a blue, velvet chair. Praying silently, she uttered, *God, please guide Dr. Stella to find whatever may be wrong with me. Whatever happens, I give it all to you. Amen.*

After fifteen minutes, a sweet, short nurse strode into the tiny area and motioned for Charlene to follow her. The lady led her into a small room where Dr. Stella waited patiently.

Greeting her, Dr. Stella said, "Hello, Charlene. What brings you here today?"

"I am having a sharp, fierce pain in my lower abdomen. I am feeling a bit tired and drowsy," Charlene quickly explained.

A dark cloud of worry thundered across Dr. Stella's face. "I might be mistaken, but I do have an idea of what could possibly be wrong with you. I would like to run a few tests to clarify my position on the matter. I don't want to jump to any assumptions before it is confirmed."

After the tests were completed, Dr. Stella swiftly guided Charlene into the waiting room while she scanned over the results. As Charlene waited impatiently, eager and scared to know the answer of the traumatizing sharpness that stung within her, she opened her black purse and pulled out her Bible. Gently flipping the precious pages, she finally came upon one of her favorite verses. "God is our refuge and strength, a very present help in trouble" (Psalms 46:1, NASB).

Peacefully she sat, hearing God whisper the gentle words to her as her heart soaked the beautiful promise in. It was as if God was sitting right next to her, holding her hand and murmuring to her that he would give her the strength to uphold this trialing journey.

Finally, the same nurse ushered Charlene into a small purple mosaic room in the back. As Charlene sat down on a soft pink bench inside the quiet room, Dr. Stella entered. A sorrowful expression spread like wild fire across Dr. Stella's pudgy face. Slowly, Dr. Stella spoke as if a tear were about to squeeze out of the corner of her sparkling, clear brown eyes. Before she began, she choked on a fiery tear. "Charlene, I have terrible news, but I also have good news. I will tell you the good news first, but please don't get too excited. Apparently, you were an expectant mother of twins."

What do you mean I was? Charlene pondered as her thoughts swirled through a maze in her mind. What was Dr. Stella saying?

"Charlene, you have had a miscarriage. It was a little baby boy. But don't worry. The other baby is perfectly fine. I am so sorry, Charlene. I know this must be difficult for you, but God has a plan and a reason for everything. You just have to trust and believe that he will lead you through this tragic time. You should thank God. Both babies could have died, but he still blessed you with one precious child. He has a wonderful plan for you, and I know you may not see it now but never give up on him. I know he will never give up on you."

The hint of hope in Charlene's heart vanished as rapid as it had developed. Slowly, a tear tickled down her cheek as she placed her hands over her face and cried out her heart's desire. It was as if the whole world had ended, and to any mother it would have as something so valuable and a part of her died away. Why would God take such a precious and innocent life away? What was happening to her? It seemed as though she were living in a drowning whirlpool that had no end. How could something good turn out of this? She lost a child, a beautiful, treasured baby. Was it her fault? Could have she saved his life in some small way?

Maybe if she had listened to Aimee and had gone to the hospital her little boy would still be alive.

Blinking the endless tears of pain away, Charlene was speechless, completely speechless. With everything in her life torn this way and that, she fled the room and ran upstairs to Todd's room. What if she lost him too? Every last bit of hope drained from within her. Her beloved husband, Nate, had died, Todd's parents had died, her sweet baby boy died, Todd was dying, and Aimee had almost died. Death seemed to surround her. What was God trying to teach her?

As Charlene abruptly turned the corner, she slipped inside Todd's dreary room. Unhurriedly, she sat on the chair next to the bed. Her heart ached to talk and spend valued time with God. She glanced out of the window at the panoramic painting below. Everything from the lilac flowers to the trees had a place. Why did God need Charlene? Did he really have a purpose and a place for her life? Suddenly, she recalled a verse that she held dear to her heart. "In Him we were also chosen, having been predestined according to the plan of Him who works out everything in conformity with the purpose of His will" (Ephesians 1:11, NIV).

God does have a plan for me. I may not feel important, and I may not be famous, but I am more valuable to God than the finest diamond. I just have to have faith in him who made all things. God is always and will always be there for me whether I know it or not. Dr. Stella is right. God will never give up on me. Why should I give up on him?

Silently, she prayed, emptying everything she felt and giving it all to God. *God, why are you doing this to me? Why are you taking away everyone in my life? I just don't understand. Everything that is decidedly the worst seems to be tossed into my life. I trust you, and I have faith that you will carry me through this, so Lord, give me hope to hold on to. I have nothing. You've taken away my Todd for the time being, and you have called my baby boy, Nathaniel, home. I am scared you are going to take everyone I love away and leave me here to suffer life alone. I don't want to think that way, but I do. Forgive me for thinking such things. I know it is not true. It just seems easier to believe that right now. Thank you for protecting this life,* she paused as she ran her hand over her large stomach. *I need somebody to love and care for, so please continue to protect my baby. And thank you for Aimee. I need her, I really do. She is a daughter to me, and I love her so much. You have brought her a long way, and I am so thankful that she desires a strong relationship with you. Give me the courage to overcome this hard strenuous battle. I know I am not alone. Thank you for being here for me. Amen.*

Grabbing Todd's hand, she held it against her face, and with the little strength she had left, she softly cried.

"Todd, I never knew that I was having twins. I just didn't know. Nathaniel, our baby boy, died, and it hurts so deeply. It feels as though I knew him personally, and now he is in heaven. We will never be able to hold him in our arms and rock him. Jesus is holding him right now, and I know Nathaniel is safe in his arms. It just hurts, Todd. Nathaniel, our precious baby boy, is gone, and you are slipping away. Don't leave me, Todd. I can't raise this baby alone. Be brave."

Her dreams and hopes vanished into thin air as anguish seized her insides. All she could do was pray that God would show his unfailing love toward her and provide her with undivided strength during this journey. It was a battle she would just have to face.

When she finally left the hospital, she clung to the steering wheel as she drove home. Suddenly, she felt a peace from God overwhelm her. She heard a voice inside her saying, "I will go before you and will be with you; I will never leave you nor forsake you. Do not be afraid; do not be discouraged" (Deuteronomy 31:8, NIV). It was God's gentle voice speaking words of truth to her soul. He would be there for her. He always was.

After parking her Durango on the driveway, she unhurriedly staggered to the front door and turned the knob. As she opened the door, she was greeted by Aimee's boisterous voice. "Auntie, how did it go? I was praying for you the entire time."

Charlene forced the mumbled words out as she choked on her tears, "I was going to have twins, but the baby boy…he…he died." It hurt to even say the words, and in complete anguish, Charlene helplessly fell into Aimee's arms. "It is all my fault. I should have let you take me to the hospital. It's all my fault!"

"No, it is not. It is not anybody's fault. It is God's plan. He has a reason. Your baby boy is safe with him. It is going to be okay."

Holding her aunt's tiny hand, Aimee softly said, "Auntie Charlene, I want to pray with you." A tiny smile formed on the corners of Charlene's lips as she squeezed her niece's hand.

Swallowing an unexpected tear, Aimee prayed, giving everything into God's hands. "Dear God, we come before you broken and in deep sorrow. We don't know why you have taken such an innocent life away, but we trust that you will show us the way. Please be with Aunt Charlene. Give her the strength to endure this unending journey. Thank you for protecting the other baby. Amen."

It was a time of sorrow Charlene would just have to withstand no matter how hard or painful it was. God would walk alongside her as she struggled through it, and he would provide the strength she needed to endure it.

The Astonishing Arrival!

As the month of August arrived, the summer's heat slowly died away, and a cool, brisk breeze replaced the cozy blanket of warmth. Aimee was finally capable of walking without her crutches with little disability. It felt so good to be able to just live without any weighing down injuries. She was free to run outside and brush her feet across the ticklish grass that coated the front yard with greenery.

Finally, the time inched closer to Charlene's awaiting due date, and she prayed wholeheartedly that God would keep the baby safe inside her. Supporting her throughout the numerous challenges that lay ahead, Charlene's parents and Sandra and her family came to visit to provide her with additional encouragement. They understood how awful it must be to suffer through so much all at one time. Charlene needed every bit of guidance that her parents and older sister brought. She couldn't raise two children on her own. She needed help, she really did.

As the eighteenth of August crawled into existence, the sun slowly arose and shone forth a bright, majestic glow. Charlene awoke from the sun gently kissing her forehead. Climbing out of bed, she swiftly slipped on a pair of jean shorts and a pink buttoned blouse. After brushing her messy hair, Charlene eagerly sauntered into the kitchen and began mixing some pancake batter.

As she placed a few strips of raw bacon into a sizzling frying pan, her mother commandingly urged, taking the batter and rapidly beating it with a wooden spoon, "You should be resting. The baby is already overdue and is going to come any day now. I don't want you overworking yourself. Sit down on the sofa, Charlene."

Instantly, Charlene ambled to the living room and wiggled into a comfortable position on the soft leather couch.

The oily bacon sputtered, and as the grease popped continuously out of the pan, Aimee strutted into the kitchen. Her long blond hair was fashioned in a side ponytail and her baby-blue eyes were delicately shimmering from the reflection of the sun.

"Good morning, Grandma. It is such a beautiful day. Did you ever realize how perfect God made everything?" Aimee grabbed the bowl of pancake mix and poured a spoonful onto another hot frying pan.

"I haven't really thought about it, dear. How was youth fellowship last night?"

"It was great. First of all, we prayed, and I prayed for Auntie Charlene and Uncle Todd. I hope I had the liberty to share some of what auntie is struggling through. God works through prayer, and prayer is what she needs."

"What did you learn about last night, if you were listening?"

"Grandma, that is the only reason I go. I don't go just because Jesse is going."

"Darling, it's just that you have something for Jesse. I saw the way you two gazed at each other when Marcy picked you up last night."

"Grandma, Jesse isn't my priority. God is the only reason I desire to go. I want to learn and grow closer to him."

"So what did you learn?" her grandmother asked as a twinkling smile spread across her aged face.

"Pastor Tom did an awesome Bible study on temptation. The study was based on a verse in Corinthians. 'No temptation has overtaken you but such as is common to man; and God is faithful, who will not allow you to be tempted beyond what you are able, but with the temptation will provide the way of escape also, so that you will be able to endure it' [1 Corinthians 10:13, NASB]. For me, I was really touched. I thought it was such an amazing verse to guide us away from sinfulness. It means that God will provide the way of escape. The way he provides is through Jesus. But God won't make us take it. We have to be the ones to choose whether or not to.

"When we are faced with a choice and Satan lures us to do the wrong thing, we are only digging a deeper hole for ourselves. God is offering his hand to us, but sometimes we don't know if we want to take it. We think what we are doing is not really that bad, and Satan continues to overthrow us. He makes things look really good on the outside, but when we open up the wrapper, there is a bitter tasting candy waiting inside. There is no sweetness. We, as people, eventually become bitter chocolates when we continue to serve the one who hates us. Satan's promises are all lies, but God's are true and just. And God loves each person no matter what they've done. Satan hates us. He just wants us to follow him instead of Christ. There is no joy in serving Satan. I know that. And I do know that serving God fulfills all our longing desires with a surpassing joy that comes only from him. He is the one worth living for."

Her grandmother's face was lit by a refreshing smile. "I want you to know how proud I am of you, Aimee. I am honored to have you as my granddaughter. You are a beautiful blossom of God's. He will use you to touch many lives."

Suddenly, Alyssa, Nick, and Tommy scampered into the kitchen and began chanting, "We are hungry! We are hungry!"

"Sit down, you three. The pancakes and bacon are all finished. Are your parents up?" their grandmother kindly asked.

Alyssa sweetly answered, "Yup, they're coming." Just then, Sandra and Matt wandered into the kitchen and sat down at the table. After everyone was seated, they held hands, and Matt asked the blessing.

In his deep, soothing voice, he softly spoke, "Dear Lord, thank you for blessing us with this delicious food. Go before us today in all we do, and be the center of the conversation on our lips. Be with Todd. I pray that in your timing he will wake up. Whatever plans you have in store for each one of us, help us to accept it and to always walk with you. In Christ's name, I pray. Amen."

Silence filled the room for almost ten minutes as everyone chomped loudly on their food. Charlene was so thankful to be with her family, especially during this time. God was definitely good.

Remembering the verse she had overheard Aimee recite that morning, Charlene whispered to herself, "No temptation has overtaken you but such as is common to man; and God is faithful, who will not allow you to be tempted beyond what you are able, but with the temptation will provide the way of escape also, so that you will be able to endure it" (1 Corinthians 10:13, NASB). She felt as though God really cared about her, and coaxing herself to forget her worries, she relied upon God to help her from being depressed. She would take the secret passageway that God had supplied for her. Instead of staying inside a dark, secluded hole, she would allow his rich promise to wash over her soul. He was here for her; he always was.

Abruptly, the clouds rolled into a deep, dark formation and soft raindrops trickled down on the earth as if it were an innocent baby crying. Tapping against the side of the house, the rain endlessly pattered on the glass windowpanes, and Charlene couldn't help but let the depression overcome her. Why was her life such a mess? Why couldn't Todd be there with her right now?

Suddenly, it struck her hard as she watched Sandra and Matt playfully tease one another while they cleaned up the dishes. Blowing sudsy soap water in his face, Sandra flirtatiously began to giggle as he immediately waltzed toward her in a welcoming embrace. Bitterness continued to encompass Charlene's serene face as she felt the hot tears surface to her eyes. It wasn't Sandra or Matt's fault that their affection for one another shone brightly to light a spark of jealousy inside Charlene. However, watching the two exchange a warmhearted hug inevitably caused Charlene to allow a feeling of sadness to sweep over her. As hard as she tried to control her emotions, she finally gave into the temptation of depression. All she grieved for was her Todd and her precious baby boy. The thought of Todd dying pierced her very being, and the tears continuously flowed down her face. Rapidly, she fled to the safe haven of her bedroom. Heavily, she cried, letting every confusing thought and feeling drain from within.

After a long moment, Aimee lightly tapped on the bedroom door, but before Charlene could answer, she walked in. Lowering herself onto the bed next to her aunt, Aimee whispered, "Everything is going to be all right. Trust in God that he will bring you through. Remember, he always does. 'Trust in the Lord with all your heart and lean not on your own understanding; in all your ways acknowledge Him and He will make your paths straight' [Proverbs 3:5–6, NIV]."

"Thank you, Aimee. God knew I needed you right now," Charlene quietly replied. Before she had a chance to regain her composure, a sharp pain seized her, and she instantaneously yelped in pain, "Ah!"

"What's wrong, Auntie?" Aimee worriedly asked. "Are you okay?"

Trying to force the words out, Charlene responded, "The baby is coming. Ah! We have to go!"

With a rush of adrenaline, Aimee yelled, "Grandma! Auntie Charlene is going into labor!"

Dashing into the bedroom, Charlene's mother frenetically scrambled into the room and assisted Charlene out to the car. "Just breathe, honey, just breathe."

"Ah! It hurts!"

"I know, dear, but everything will be all right," her mother affirmed as she climbed inside the vehicle next to Charlene. Aimee and Sandra instantly followed and hopped inside the car while the rest of the family remained at the house.

Before long, Sandra, Charlene's mother, and Aimee were at the hospital, waiting impatiently to hear news back of Charlene's delivery. She had been taken in immediately upon their arrival to the infirmary. Now all they had to do was wait.

Excitement filled Aimee with exuberant rushes as the thought of having her very first brother or sister entered her mind. It was absolutely thrilling.

"Dear God, give my mom, Charlene, the strength to get through this time. Protect the baby and my mom with your undivided care. Amen," Aimee softly said, placing her tiny hand on her grandma who was shivering and shaking with fear. "The baby and my mom will be fine. Just trust in God. He knows everything."

"I know, dear. It just seems like she's been in there forever," her grandmother quivered. Suddenly, it registered, and her grandma couldn't help but ask, "Aimee, did you call Charlene your mother?"

Smiling, Aimee answered, "She has been my mom ever since she adopted me. She has taught me the principles of life, and I have learned so much from her. If I hadn't come to live here, I probably wouldn't have accepted Christ as my personal Lord and Savior. The orphanage was awful. There was no love there whatsoever. I always felt like I was alone, but God was so good to me, and he blessed me with a true mother, my auntie Charlene. Living here has been the best thing that has ever happened to me. Auntie Charlene has always been my mother and forever will be."

A glaze of tears shone in Sandra's eyes as she softly uttered, "Aimee, you are so lucky to have Charlene as your mother."

"I know I am."

The awaiting hours ahead were unknown, but God had the beautiful plan all worked out. He knew the time and place and every single detail that would transpire to fulfill his glorious plan. How it was going to turn out no one else knew, but during the time of waiting, they prayed continuously for the safety of Charlene and the astonishing new arrival.

As the time passed, Dr. Stella finally waltzed into the waiting room and announced, "Charlene and her beautiful baby girl are perfectly fine. You can come see them if you'd like."

Exuberantly, they followed Dr. Stella into a light-brown room.

"Thank you, God, for keeping them safe. You are wonderful and an amazing God. Amen," Aimee murmured under her breath.

Managing a smile, Charlene stared at her family, a carefree glow lighting her face. If only Todd had been there to see their beautiful baby girl. She was the cutest baby Charlene had ever seen. She had deep chocolate brown eyes with crisp black hair outlining her sweet face. Todd would be so proud to be a daddy. He absolutely loved children, and now he had one of his own.

Slowly, Aimee lowered herself onto the bed next to her aunt. Staring into her aunt's green eyes, she quietly asked, "Auntie Charlene, is it okay if I call you mom?"

A tear slipped down Charlene's cheek as a smile evolved onto her face. "Aimee, I would be honored if you called me your mother." Embracing her tightly, Charlene held Aimee in her arms. It was the moment Aimee had been waiting for her entire life. She had never really had a mother who loved and cared for her. Now, she did.

After a long moment, Aimee gently said, "Could I hold my new baby sister?"

Placing the small, warm bundle into her arms, Charlene watched as Aimee gazed at the wee one sleeping peacefully. Never in her life had Aimee held a baby before, but by the way she rocked her back and forth, no one would have been able to guess that she hadn't. It was the first time in a long time that Charlene realized that God's timing was the perfect timing. He had blessed Charlene and Todd with a beautiful angel. Not everything in life was joyous, but the moments of joy that God gave them were times to cherish.

Sweet Sixteen

The months slowly passed as the frigid month of December evolved. It had been a little over a year since Todd's serious accident, and there was no sign of improvement whatsoever. The baby was now three and a half months old and was perfectly healthy. Although earlier on Charlene had intended on calling their newborn baby Grace, she suddenly changed her mind. While she was reading her Bible one day, she stumbled across a beautiful verse. "Behold, children are a gift of the Lord, the fruit of the womb is a reward" (Psalm 127:3, NASB). It comforted her to know that their baby was a prized possession from God, a miracle. After soaking in the heartening words, Charlene had no other choice but to name the baby Miracle. With all that had happened, truly little Miracle was a blessing from God.

Aimee thoroughly enjoyed Miracle too. She always pitched in to help whenever she could. She had really grown fond of home schooling, and she especially loved being with Miracle. Besides, Miracle was her very first sibling.

It was the beginning of December, and the first snowfall layered the busy streets of Edmonton with a thin envelop of tiny flakes. Christmas was just around the corner, and decorations were strewn every which way. Christmas lights were being draped across rooftops while evergreen trees were being ornamented with colorful embellishments inside. It was such a beautiful, joyous time of year—the celebration of Jesus Christ's birth.

As Charlene trudged up the winding staircase to Todd's quiet hospital room, she lugged the heavy baby seat that held Miracle in tightly. Slowly, she grinned down at the tiny girl smiling up at her. Even though Miracle was only three and a half months old, she was such a happy little baby.

As Charlene scampered into the dark, dreary room, she sat down in a light-blue chair and gently lifted Miracle out of her seat. With precise care, Charlene laid Miracle on the soft bed next to Todd. Miracle's chocolate-brown eyes focused in on her daddy who was sleeping soundly. Rapidly, she waved her tiny arms before slowly placing her small hand in her daddy's palm.

"Todd, this is your new baby girl, Miracle. She looks so much like you. Her hair has lightened to a dark shade of brown now, but she has your eyes. I know you would be proud. She is her daddy's little girl." Charlene saw the resemblance between the two. The way Miracle stared up at him it was as if she knew exactly who he was. He was her daddy.

As Charlene reached to pick Miracle up, the unique beat of a cell phone buzzed, and she abruptly answered it, "Hello."

"Hi, Mom, it's Aimee."

"If you are wondering how long I will be, I should only be here for another half hour."

"Actually, I was wondering if I could go to Karla's sweet sixteenth slumber party tonight. Youth was cancelled, so Karla decided to quickly plan her birthday party."

"That's fine with me, Aimee. Just make sure you're home before three in the afternoon. We are driving up to Calgary tomorrow for Nick's fourteenth birthday, and your grandparents are going to be there."

"Okay, will do. Thanks, Mom," Aimee articulated as she hung up the phone. Quickly, she tossed some clothes and cosmetics in a black bag before reaching for her jacket.

After she finished packing, she scrambled outside toward her mother's beat-up car that sat helplessly in ruins. As she backed the white junker out of the driveway, she steered it into the direction of the Stanford's farm, feeling every bump she passed over. The Stanford's log house was incomparably small to the vastness that surrounded them. Close to twenty horses moseyed lazily across the field, munching on the stacks of hay.

When she finally arrived, Tiffany and Brandy were rolling out their sleeping bags. Although there were a lot of girls Aimee did not know, she recognized a few of them from when she attended the public school.

"Aimee, I am so happy that you are here. You can put your stuff beside mine and Tiffany's. We don't know anybody else either," Brandy screamed with excitement as her long light-brown hair rustled from side to side.

Instantly, Aimee positioned her suitcase next to Tiffany's and swiftly unrolled her black-and-blue sleeping bag overtop of the caramel colored carpet.

After everybody arrived, Marcy invited the girls into the small kitchen for supper where everyone crowded around an oak table. Brandy and Tiffany immediately slid onto the solid maple bench next to another girl and began a random conversation. It seemed more challenging for Aimee to become involved in the discussion, so she sat there quietly to herself.

As she stared widely at the many strangers, scared to share her opinion, Jesse suddenly sat down next to her and softly asked, "How is homeschooling? You are in grade eleven, right?"

"Yes, I am. I really love being at home especially now that Miracle is born. To be honest, this year is definitely not as challenging as last year was."

He glared at her for a moment as if he misunderstood her.

"Oh, the workload is harder for sure. I just mean that now that I am a Christian and Jesus is my personal Savior, I don't face the same difficulties as I did before."

"That is so good to hear. With Jesus, life has a lot more to do with him and a lot less to do with us if you know what I mean. I can't wait to graduate this year. I mean I have waited so long for this moment."

Suddenly, Aimee realized that she had completely forgotten about Jesse's graduation. How could have the thought slipped her mind?

In front of everyone, Jesse continued chatting with Aimee not seeming to mind some of the girls taking notice of them. "Well, you know me. I am just getting ready to throw the schoolbooks away and open God's Word. This coming year I am planning on going to His Hill in Texas, and I suppose the year after I'll go to college. I want to become a policeman, God willing."

"Someday I hope to attend Bible school too."

Shocked by her response, Jesse blurted, "Really? I wasn't sure if you would. I think that is so awesome." Swiftly, he inched closer to her so only she could interpret the words that he whispered, "I am not big on proms or anything, but just to let you know if I was, I would have definitely asked you, princess."

The sweet, gentle words replayed over and over again in her mind as she thought intensely about what he had just said. He was the sweetest and sincerest guy she had ever met. His kind personality reflected his image. He was a good-looking, down-to-earth kind of a guy. It felt like a beautiful dream that she never wanted to wake up from.

The reason why his words had touched her heart so much was because many months ago during their first enchanting walk through the park, Jesse had told her that she was a princess of the King. It was beautiful to think she was a child of God, absolutely beautiful.

As she zoned back into the present, the homemade pizza was served, the aroma scenting the kitchen.

&

Charlene decidedly stayed with Todd the entire night. As she cradled Miracle in her arms, the tiny one closed her eyes and fell fast asleep. Gently, Charlene laid her in the baby seat on the floor. Rocking it lightly, Charlene finally became too weary to keep her strained eyes open any longer, and she solemnly fell into a deep sleep. She gripped Todd's strong, muscular hand tightly in her own. He would wake up eventually, wouldn't he?

&

When the girls finished watching two chic flick movies, they settled on playing "truth or dare."

"Aimee, truth or dare?" Karla asked, her eyes wide with exhilaration.

"I guess I'll pick truth."

The mischievous twinkle in Karla's eyes shone wildly. Knowing she had scrimmaged through her deep thoughts for the one perfect question, Karla finally shrieked, "Aimee, you have to tell the truth. Do you like my brother, Jesse?"

Slightly embarrassed, Aimee's cheeks flushed a pinkish red, and she didn't dare reveal her secret to the whole world. Rapidly, she answered, "Of course not. Why would you ask such a thing?"

Laughing unbearably, Karla responded, "Because did you see the way you fluttered your baby-blue eyes at him when he talked to you at the supper table tonight?"

A girl named Natalia added, "And the way you looked at him with dignity and respect, as if you two were the only people in this world."

It was almost as if everyone in the room could tell that she was being deceitful.

"Fine, I like Jesse. What's the big deal?"

Tiffany jumped right into the conversation and exclaimed, "Because it's not that hard to tell that he likes you too. He is practically in love with you, Aimee. Wake up, girl!"

Sarcastically, Mandy said, "Jesse likes Aimee? Yah right. I think he was just being nice to her. He is like that to a lot of girls."

"Mandy, you are just jealous that Jesse likes Aimee and not you. If you ask me, you are the one that should wake up," Natalia commented.

"Natalia, you don't even know Jesse as well as I do," Mandy rudely stated.

"Okay, I think that Karla knows her brother the best. Karla, does Jesse treat every girl the same way he treats Aimee?" Brandy curiously asked.

"Actually, he doesn't. Of course he is nice to other girls, but he definitely talks about Aimee more than any of them. I am pretty sure that he likes her if it is not obvious enough," Karla confirmed.

Aimee felt like the center of attention for the rest of the evening as the girls kept asking questions and commenting about her relationship with Jesse.

At around one o'clock in the morning, Marcy marched quietly into the living room and asked nicely for the girls to simmer down. Like a hot, boiling cup of coffee, the girls sizzled down as they drifted off into a dazzling, dreamy sleep. They would chitchat more in the morning. Besides, at around ten o'clock, they were planning on going horseback riding through the snowy trails. The day ahead was full of unexpected memories none of them would ever forget.

The Ride

As the sun glittered through the large windows like streams of confetti, it gleamed over the girls who were still sound asleep. Marcy crept in quietly, trying not to make a peep. Softly, she whispered, "Girls, it's time to get up. You guys are going horseback riding in an hour and a half. Breakfast will be ready in fifteen minutes."

With that, she trampled out of the living room and into the light-brown painted kitchen. Immediately after Marcy disappeared, the girls raced to the bathrooms to get ready for the awaiting day. Applying makeup and fixing their hair, the fourteen girls squished into the three bathrooms that were available. Aimee quickly brushed her long blond hair and braided it, tying it with two pink stretchy elastics. As she finished smearing on her makeup, she gathered her cosmetics and placed them inside her suitcase.

Scampering into the kitchen, Aimee swiftly slid next to Natalia who had shoulder length auburn hair and an overall thin-shaped figure. She looked like a super model in a fashion show.

Leaning over, Natalia murmured, "You are the girl who likes Jesse, right?"

Aimee smiled sheepishly, hoping her face didn't appear as warm as it felt. Before long, it would be broadcasted on the news.

After ten minutes, Brandy strutted into the kitchen as her silky, light-brown hair swished vigorously. Quickly, she fastened it into a tight ponytail as she plopped down next to Aimee. "Did you see him yet?"

Confusion filled Aimee's mind as she nervously asked, "Who?"

Laughing hysterically, Brandy replied, "Your boyfriend, silly!"

As Brandy finished the statement, Jesse, oblivious to what was happening, strolled into the noisy room. Aimee's cheeks flushed a rosy pink, and she rapidly nudged Brandy's arm. Hopefully, he hadn't heard their conversation. How embarrassing!

Opening her stiff, crusty eyes, Charlene abruptly awoke. As she glanced at her black watch, she noticed the numbers continuously flashing 11:03 a.m. How could have she slept in so late? Why didn't Miracle cry? Slowly, she peered to where she had carefully placed the baby seat on the floor. The tiny seat was still in its original place, yet something was missing.

Finally, everything registered. Where was her precious little angel? The little tike didn't just walk away; she was only three and a half months with no capability of escaping whatsoever. Where could she be? Charlene's heart stopped beating and everything inside her collapsed. Searching frantically, barely receiving a single ounce of air, Charlene closely examined Todd's room, under the bed, in the bathroom, and behind small obstacles. There was no trace of her anywhere.

After she finished her scouting, she scampered down the stairs to the front desk. How in the world was she going to find her precious baby in such a huge building? Had some stranger kidnapped her?

Bowing her head as she patiently waited for the lady at the front desk to assist her, Charlene quickly whispered a prayer, "God, be with my precious baby. Protect her and lead me to where she is. In Christ's name, I pray. Amen."

No matter how long it would take for her to find Miracle she would not lose faith. God would bring her through. He always did.

ꙮ

As Tiffany joyously waltzed into the tiny kitchen, she shot her piercing brown eyes at Aimee. "Awe, why aren't you sitting beside Jesse, you two lovebirds?" Tiffany whispered.

Aimee had had enough of all the ewes and awes. Last night it was fun to have all the attention, but now she was getting sick and tired of it.

After everyone gulped down some fresh-squeezed orange juice and filled their rumbling stomachs with bacon and breakfast sausage, Jesse led all of the perky girls outside and into the horse stable. The stench was horrifying as Aimee trudged inside, and she immediately plugged her nose. How could anyone stand that awful smell?

Precisely, Jesse arranged each girl with a beautiful horse to ride. When it was Aimee's turn, he handed her the reigns of a black horse that had tints of Cimarron in its shiny coat, one of the most beautiful horses the Stanford's owned. Karla glanced at Tiffany, and both girls knew that Jesse had given his own horse to Aimee. Awe, how romantic! The girls giggled as they passed by on their horses.

As Aimee attempted to mount the horse, Jesse softly asked, "Do you need some help getting on Diesel?"

What if everyone saw him helping her? All the girls would make more remarks on how much Jesse and she were meant for each other, that is, except for Mandy. With all she had in her, she pulled herself up, and as she swung her leg over the saddle, she slipped and fell backwards. As she descended, Jesse reached over and caught her before she hit the hard-dirt ground.

"Thank you," she said shyly.

Grinning wildly, he snatched a wooden stool from the corner of the barn, so she could stand on it.

"I wonder if he would do that for me," Brandy whispered to Karla.

"Probably not. You should see him after youth. All he talks about is Aimee, Aimee, and more about Aimee. Sometimes it gets really old."

❧

When the tall, slim lady finished filing some papers, Charlene nervously questioned, "Excuse me, I don't mean to bother you, but I am looking for my baby. My husband Todd is in a terrifying state of a coma. I spent the night here, and when I woke up this morning, my baby, Miracle, was gone. I am so frightened. Have you seen a baby at all? She has dark-brown curly hair and brown-chocolate eyes. My husband is in room 219 on the fourth floor."

The lady's voice suddenly changed to a tender and gentle tone. "Didn't one of the nurses tell you?"

What? She was so confused. What was going on? What had happened to her baby?

❧

After the fourteen girls and Jesse were settled on their horses, Karla led the way up into the thick underbrush. As the sun brightly shone, the group plodded through the deep snow. It looked like a delicious cake with white frosting layering the top. The sun glazed down on them, and the heat evaporated some of the chill that stung the air. Aimee was at the end of the train of horses due to her mishap while mounting. Frustrated, she tugged on Diesel's reigns. He ate everything in sight, filling his hungry stomach with the dry greenery that poked its head from out of the snow. Impatiently, Aimee stammered, "Diesel, if you eat anymore, you will get so fat that you won't be able to move. Now move it, please."

As she dug her heels into the side of the horse to inch Diesel forward, Jesse rode up behind her. "I suppose that is one way to talk to a horse. But I'd suggest just gripping the reigns tighter. Don't give him as much lead rope. That way he won't be able to eat everything." Jesse winked at her.

Stretching in the distance, an open field with no forestry extended from west to east. As Karla approached the spacious pastureland, she nudged Smoky forward, and her horse began galloping gracefully. The rest of the horses followed smoothly behind except for Diesel. He just stopped and stared at the herd of horses in the distance.

"It's all that food you ate, Diesel," Aimee moaned, booting Diesel in the side.

"Hey, Aimee, if you stop kicking him so hard, he will just follow in line behind the other horses. Whistle to get him moving."

She perched her lips and blew, but it was no use; she was practically just blowing air. All of a sudden, she heard a gentle voice tenderly speaking to Diesel. "Come on, boy. That's it, come on." Jesse whistled, and Diesel fixed himself into an easygoing gallop.

Close to the front of the pack, Tiffany guided a gorgeous brown horse with black velvet socks and shiny hair. When she glanced back, she caught a glimpse of Jesse and Aimee riding together. "Brandy, I have something to tell you." Tiffany yanked on the reigns until Candy Cane slowed down to a comfortably paced trot.

Instantly, Brandy directed a beautiful black stallion toward Tiffany.

"Brandy, did you see Jesse and Aimee? They are so cute together."

"Yes, I did. They are so adorable. They really are perfect for each other."

As the two girls giggled, they glimpsed back, and their laughter immediately subsided. Instantaneously, Brandy and

Tiffany noticed what had happened, and in a flash they turned their horses around and galloped toward the scene.

"Aimee, are you okay?" Jesse timorously asked as he quickly dismounted Skittles and reached for Aimee's hand.

Tiffany halted Candy Cane and softly questioned, "What happened?"

"Diesel accidentally tripped on a huge rock and bucked Aimee off. She went sprawling in the air," Jesse explained.

Aimee closed her eyes as she suddenly realized the sharp pain in her left leg. "My leg, it hurts."

Lifting Aimee in his muscular grasp, Jesse held her in his arms and began walking home.

"Jesse, it is way too far to walk all the way back home," Karla demanded.

He ignored his sister and continued trampling through the snow. It made Karla angrier when Jesse disregarded her advice.

Slowly, Karla snatched Skittles reigns and tied them to the horn on her polished, black saddle. The group headed for home, and sadness streamed through Karla's soul. It was only five minutes away to a beautiful spring full of rocks and tiny currents forcing the clear water forward. It was such a beautiful sight created by God. It was like a perfect painting with absolutely no mistakes on it. How could anyone not believe God existed? His hand was upon the entire earth and still people didn't believe in him. How could such a detailed panoramic picture be so perfect? It wouldn't be perfect without the one true and perfect God. In fact, the earth wouldn't have existed at all without God.

Quickly as if Karla dismissed her thought life, she politely asked, "Mandy, could you tie Diesel's reigns to your saddle horn?"

Grabbing the beautiful horse's ropes, Mandy fastened them tightly around her horn. Jealously strewn through her soul as if it was a deathly sickness; she was definitely envious of Jesse's little crush on Aimee. Why did Jesse have to like Aimee? Why couldn't he just like her?

The Promise

As the lady behind the large desk explained to Charlene what had happened, it seemed as if the world was coming to an abrupt end. Clearly, all Charlene could make out was people silently bustling around the hospital; she could not hear a single word. Finally, as Charlene managed to zone back into the present, she kindly asked, "Could you repeat that? I am sorry it is just that I can't seem to focus very well right now."

So much had gone on in her short life, and at the time being, she didn't understand why. Yet God had a special reason and plan for her existence. It would just take time as she journeyed through the mysterious, winding valleys of life. God would be her stronghold; she just needed to reach out her hand and slip it into his comforting grip. He would never let her go.

"Well, ma'am, an advanced nurse elucidated to me that your baby is being treated. Two nurses checked on your husband early this morning. They noticed the baby's face turning a peachy red. Dr. Jens is looking after her for the time being. I am afraid that your baby is having difficulty breathing. If those nurses hadn't been there when they were, your darling little girl would have died. Follow me. I will show you where your daughter is."

The woman swiftly led Charlene up four flights of stairs and down the crowded hall. As Charlene entered Todd's room, she noticed two nurses and Dr. Jens carefully hooking medical cords to Miracle to assist her in her breathing.

"I am sure the little tike will not need it for long. Miracle is completely fine. We are very sorry nobody told you. You looked so tired and worn out; we didn't want to worry you anymore," one of them gently said. Worry her? It scared her even more to know her baby had disappeared.

For a brief moment, the shock overpowered Charlene, and she was unable to respond. Slowly, she lowered herself onto the chair in the corner as she quietly uttered, "Do you mind if I hold my baby?"

After placing Miracle in Charlene's arms, the nurses promptly strutted out of the room. As a tear slid down her cheek, Charlene held Miracle's tiny hands in her own. She didn't know what she would have done if the sweet ladies hadn't checked in on Todd when they had. Miracle would have slipped away without her knowing, and she wouldn't have been able to do anything about it.

"Dear God, thank you for saving my precious baby's life. I don't know what I would have done without her. She and Aimee are one of the only reasons I am fighting this battle, struggling through this unending journey. I probably would have given up a long time ago if it weren't for them. I surrender all I am to you, Lord. You are my rock and my fortress and my deliverer. Amen."

Slowly, she cradled Miracle tightly in her arms and held her close to her chest, afraid she might stop breathing otherwise. Within minutes, Mira was fast asleep. Everything would be all right. God would be there for Charlene; he always was.

Glancing up, Charlene stared at Todd who was lying on the bed helplessly, unable to do anything. Oh, how she wished he would awake. It would be Christmas soon, and Todd would most likely not be there to spend the joyous occasion with her. As long as he was at least here in the hospital, everything would be as normal as it had been lately. She just prayed that he wouldn't leave her here to raise their child alone. They needed him, Aimee, Miracle, and she.

Gazing out the window that welcomed the warmth of the sunshine in, she noticed tiny snowflakes delicately descend from the heavens. She couldn't help but wonder what this Christmas season would bring forth.

⸙

As the horses trudged on slowly, the snow sprinkled softly to the ground. It was getting cooler as every minute passed. Silence filled the brisk December air as Jesse hurriedly walked, carrying Aimee in his muscular arms.

Mandy tugged on the reigns and guided her horse next to the gorgeous stallion Brandy was riding. "I wonder if he would carry me if I hurt my leg. There is probably nothing wrong with Aimee anyways. I bet she is just pretending so he'll hold her in his arms."

Muttering under her breath, Brandy sputtered, "I don't think so. She already crushed her left leg in a car accident several months ago. I don't believe that Aimee would ruin everyone else's time just because she wanted to be near Jesse."

"Whatever! I think she would. That is the kind of person Aimee appears to be," Mandy puffed.

Finally, the little farmhouse in the distance came into view. Karla whistled, and Smoky swiftly cantered toward the house at a smooth pace. "I'll go get my mom. She can drive you to the hospital, Aimee," Karla hollered behind her. As she neared the house, she rapidly dismounted her white, brown paint horse and darted toward the front door. "Mom, come quick. Aimee's hurt real bad."

Rushing outside, Marcy emerged from the house as she slipped her winter jacket on. "What happened?"

"Diesel tripped and bucked her off the saddle. She injured her left leg, the same one she had broken earlier in the accident," Karla explained.

"Does your leg hurt, dear?"

Aimee nodded as she winced in pain. It felt like she was going to die. The shivers started crawling through her body, and she knew she was going into shock.

After Marcy shoved the keys into the ignition and backed the mini van out of the driveway, Jesse carefully transferred Aimee from his arms into the warm, toasty vehicle.

"Karla, stay here with the rest of your friends and unsaddle the horses. We shouldn't be too long," Marcy strictly commanded.

Tiffany, Brandy, and Mandy instantly scooted into the back of the white van while Aimee and Jesse occupied the middle row. As Jesse closed the door, Marcy rapidly shifted gears and maneuvered the vehicle through the icy layers of snow.

Upon their arrival at the hospital, Marcy steered the van in front of the emergency doors. "Jesse, run up to the fourth floor to see if Charlene is visiting Todd. The room number is 219. If she isn't, could you give her a call? I am sure you know their number off by heart."

"I am sure you do, Jesse. Hint, hint," Tiffany giggled.

After Jesse carefully lifted Aimee inside the hospital's welcoming care and gently placed her in a waiting chair, he scampered up four flights of winding stairs. Directing his steps into room 219, he immediately noticed two nurses unhooking an oxygen tank from Miracle. As the ladies finished, Charlene uttered, "Thank you for saving my baby's life. I am most grateful."

"You are welcome. God placed us there at the right time. His timing is always perfect," a sweet nurse articulated before scurrying out of the room.

Charlene pondered the statement, '*God's timing is always perfect.' It was, wasn't it? If it was God's purpose that Todd would eventually wake up, then it was meant to be, but if Todd's life was meant to end, then God had a reason. Everything would work out all in his timing.*

"Mrs. Carter, you have to come quick. Aimee is in the emergency hall. We went horseback riding this morning, all of Karla's friends of course, and Aimee's horse tripped. She was bucked off, and I think she broke her left leg again,"Jesse asserted, interrupting Charlene's beautiful thoughts.

Immediately, Charlene stood up, and a cloud of worry evolved upon her face. "Show me where she is?"

Jesse guided Charlene down the stairs and into the emergency ward. As they strutted into the waiting room, Mandy, Tiffany, and Brandy came to meet them.

"Aimee went in room 307 with Karla's mom and the doctor. He said from the way it looks he thinks that her leg is most likely broken. He also said that you could go in there whenever you got here,"Tiffany finished with her usual perkiness, although by the edge of her voice, they could tell she was just as afraid as they were.

"Could you hold Miracle, Tiffany?"

Tiffany nodded as Charlene gently transferred the little one into her arms. Immediately, Charlene bravely marched into the room where Aimee patiently waited.

After Charlene talked with the doctor, the trio emerged from the quiet room. There, Aimee stood hunched over metal crutches.

"Auntie Charlene, I still want to go to Calgary today. I'll be fine."

"Aimee, it is a long drive. I think I'll just phone Sandra and tell her what happened. She'll understand. We'll just stay here in Edmonton for the weekend," Charlene responded.

"Girls, let's go get the van," Marcy urged, and the three girls instantly followed her outside. Willingly, Jesse waited with Aimee while Charlene retrieved the Durango.

"Are you sure you're going to be okay? I am so sorry about your leg. I feel like it is partially my fault. Diesel is my horse, you know,"Jesse murmured.

Aimee answered softly, “It was just an accident. I could have fallen off Skittles too. It’s not your fault at all. I want to thank you for carrying me back to your house and making sure I was okay. It meant a lot to me.”

A bright, glimmering smile shone across his face as he replied, “It was my pleasure to help a really good and special friend. You know, you mean everything to me, and I promise I will always be here for you.”

“You promise?”

“I promise, princess.”

When Charlene and Aimee arrived home, a strange vehicle was parked on the driveway. It was a white Chevrolet truck. Swiftly, Charlene helped Aimee out of the Durango and gently pulled Mira out of her car seat. A mist hung in the air, and the cold air lapped against Charlene’s face. Glancing at the license plate on the Chevy truck, the code suddenly registered in Charlene’s mind. She was absolutely speechless. As two figures scrambled out of the truck toward her, a tear rolled down Charlene’s face.

“Mom and Dad, what are you doing here?”

“Charlene, we haven’t seen you in over two years. We have been thinking about you lately,” her mother-in-law enthusiastically verbalized. Kathie had light-brown eyes and a dark shade of auburn hair. She was a beautiful woman with such a gentle and kind way about her.

Inviting them inside the warm abode, the four of them huddled around the kitchen table and sipped on hot cups of cocoa.

“Mom and Dad, this is Aimee, my niece. She came to live with me about nine months ago. And Aimee, this is my first husband’s parents.”

“Mom, I didn’t know you were married before.”

“Yes, Nate died a while ago. Then I married your uncle Todd.”

“We just heard about Todd. I am so sorry. You have gone through so much, Charlene. We have been praying for you,” Kathie sympathetically said.

"Well, thank you. I need prayer right now. And this is Miracle. She was born in August," Charlene smiled as she cradled the newborn in her arms.

"Todd is the luckiest man alive. He has such a beautiful daughter and wife," Kathie pronounced.

"Would you like to hold her?"

"Yes, I would," Kathie uttered as Charlene gently transitioned Mira into Kathie's arms.

"We are just passing through, and we thought it would be nice to drop in and see you. We are visiting Kathie's sister for the weekend," her father-in-law interrupted. Bill was a thin, short man with detailed features. His eyes were a deep, distinct brown, and his hair was slightly grey. Finally, he continued, "Charlene, there is a reason why we are here. Just yesterday I found a letter."

"A letter?" Charlene was completely confused. Who was the letter from?

"Yes, it is a letter from Nate. I found it in my office drawer. It's addressed to you." Bill promptly handed the envelope to Charlene.

The tears stung her eyes, and she slowly unfolded the piece of paper. Memories of Nate flooded her mind as she read the note.

My Beautiful Charlene,

I wish with all my heart we could have spent more time together. You are so special and dear to me. I have written this letter to you because I know my life is at risk every time I depart our house to leave for work. Don't ever hesitate to call God. He will always be there for you, Charlene; he was always there for me. His steadfast promise, "The Lord Himself goes before you and will be with you; He will never leave you nor forsake you. Do not be afraid; do not be discouraged" (Deuteronomy 31:8, niv). Never lose faith in him because he never loses faith in you. You don't need to worry about today. You need to face tomorrow and know we will be reunited in eternity. No matter where I am, I will always love you. It hurts me to know you are reading this because I am no longer here with you. You made all my days bright when they would've been dark. Take care, my beautiful.

With all my love,
Nate

P.S. I hope the enclosed money will help you live for a while. The thought of possibly dying pierced me to think I would leave you with nothing. My desire has always been to protect and care for you. When I was a boy, I saved up all my hard-earned money because I didn't need nor desire anything. Well, God had a special purpose for me doing that. It is for you; all I have is yours. You are everything to me and waiting for you was worth it. No baseball glove or hockey stick could ever replace you. You are the most beautiful woman I have ever known, and I love you more than life itself. Take care, my beautiful.

A roll of hundred dollar bills fell out of the envelope and onto the floor. It felt as if Charlene had just lost Nate. He was a wonderful man; he truly was. The overwhelming tears slipped from the corner of her eyes. "I can't keep this money."

"Nate would have wanted you to, dear. I know my son, and he loved you more than anything. Keep it," Kathie insisted as she tugged on Bill's sleeve. "Darling, we should be leaving."

"Thank you for stopping in. I really appreciate it. Take care." Charlene slowly arose from the table and embraced Kathie. "I wish you could have stayed longer, I really do."

"Good-bye, Charlene. Aimee it was nice meeting you. You take care of your aunt now. She is going to need it. Good-bye, little Miracle." Kathie gently handed Miracle back to Charlene.

As Charlene waved from the window, the Chevy truck rolled down the road and into the thick fog that blanketed the air. She was in complete shock from the entire situation. It was too much for her right now.

"I am going to my room, Aimee. Could you watch Mira? I have so much to think about."

"For sure, Mom. It is a lot for me too. I didn't know that you were married before Uncle Todd."

"Yes, I was, and it's almost as if he was still here." Hurriedly, Charlene retired to her quiet, dark room and read the letter over and over again. It was a long night as the tears swelled up in her eyes. Oh, how she missed Nate and Todd. What would come of all this?

The Mysterious Stranger

As January quickly passed, February rolled around. The snow was starting to leave the prairie-like city as the sunshine melt the fluffy comforters away. Some days seemed to fly by so fast, while others seemed to drag on endlessly. In the middle of March, Miracle started talking, none of which anyone could understand, but it was cute to hear her babble on as if everyone could interpret what she was saying.

Slowly, spring revealed its beginning as the flowers bloomed along the prairie patches. It was the month of May, and the sun brought forth an endless glow.

As Aimee's seventeenth birthday unraveled, her grandparents chipped into the affordable expense of a well-conditioned old car. How thrilled with joy Aimee was to finally have her very own vehicle. She was so grateful to her grandparents. They really didn't need too, but they insisted. They had really grown fond of Aimee. It seemed as though she had always been a genuine part of the family.

On her birthday, May fourteenth, Jesse had taken Aimee out for a romantic dinner at the finest restaurant, and he had bought her a beautiful diamond necklace. It was absolutely the most thoughtful gift she had ever received. In her heart, she could not deny that Jesse truly cared for her, and as much as she tried, she couldn't dismiss her own feelings. She was falling for him, no matter which way she looked at it.

She had managed a part-time job at the Murphy's store. They had seen a huge change in her attitude and barely recognized she was the same girl. She had really matured, and now she was sprouting into a beautiful godly woman. Every day she was getting prettier and prettier, her long blond hair flowing like a peaceful waterfall descending into its banks and her baby-blue eyes shining as bright as the lustrous sky.

Every now and then, Mandy would attend youth group with Karla and her friends. Nobody knew, but Mandy had a secret crush on Jesse. Brandy and Tiffany suspected it every time Jesse talked to Aimee. They could see the nasty, evil glares Mandy shot Aimee's way. Of course, Aimee just brushed them off and continued her conversation. Tiffany and Brandy didn't doubt it was because Jesse paid no attention to Mandy whatsoever.

On the final roundup of youth before summer, Karla, Tiffany, Aimee, Brandy, and Mandy participated in the deep discussion.

"You guys are sleeping over at my house after, right?" Karla whispered.

"That is the plan," Tiffany blurted. Her dark-blond hair was styled in a side ponytail, and her chocolate-brown eyes popped from the slight makeup she was wearing.

On the drive back to Karla's house, the five girls discussed what they had learned. It was wonderful to be able to talk about God with other Christian girls. Mandy, of course, wasn't a Christian, but she was beginning to piece together what Christianity really was.

When the white mini van screeched to a halt in front of their small farmhouse, the girls hurriedly jumped out and skipped lightheartedly up the front steps. Anxiously, they sat on the comfortable floor in the living room, each holding a cup of cold orange juice. The amber sunset outside reflected off the windows, and the dim moon was peaking from behind the clouds. Soon the entire sky would be a majestic royal-blue with tiny flickering diamonds scattered throughout.

For a moment, silence rang in the air, and finally, Mandy nervously asked, “I was wondering if you guys could help me become a Christian. I am not exactly sure how to ask him. I have learned so much about God, and I am really yearning to have a relationship with him, the way you guys do.”

After the four girls guided Mandy through the wonderful process of receiving the Lord as her personal Savior, they began sharing the amazing things that God had done in their own lives.

“God has been so awesome. I have had so many rough experiences, but I am glad that God has forgiven me, and it is all behind me now. My dad died when I was six years old, and my mom passed away when I was fourteen. It was such a difficult time in my life. I was angry at God even though I had no right to be. It wasn't his fault in any way. He would have comforted me if only I had let him, but I was too stubborn. Fortunately, my aunt Charlene adopted me, and although it has been a hard journey, it is reassuring to know I am not walking it alone. Some days are beautiful while some days are dreary, but it doesn't matter because God will always be there for me. I love knowing he will never leave me nor forsake me. It is such an amazing promise,” Aimee exclaimed.

“I always thought that your aunt was your real mother. You guys act like you share a normal mother-daughter relationship,” Mandy muttered.

Aimee had never really had a mother before Charlene, but she decided to keep that part concealed deep down in her heart. Her real mother had always been gone and never had attended to the needs of her family. Her father had been the only reason her mother had kept living. But after he died, it was like she died inside too. In time, Aimee was finally able to cherish the moments of having a true mother. And for some special reason, God had placed Charlene as that loving person in Aimee's life.

"That is the best part. My aunt has always treated me as her very own daughter. She never favors Miracle over me. God knew I needed a mother, and my aunt was the perfect match. It truly is amazing how God works." Aimee smiled as she swallowed some sweet, delicious juice.

"Brandy, you never really talk about your dad. Where does he work?" Karla curiously asked.

"He used to be a firefighter, but he quit about two and a half years ago."

"What happened?" Tiffany's face flushed a look of concern as her eyes clouded over with tears.

"There was a fire on twenty-third street downtown. Four kids were trapped inside the burning building, and three firefighters scuttled inside in search of them. After they were rescued, my dad realized that his partner, Rick, was still inside. Nathaniel and my dad rushed back in without delay and found Rick unconscious. My dad said that a wooden board had fallen and hit Rick's head. Rapidly, my dad carried Rick back through the maze of flames. As he glanced back, he saw Nathaniel trapped behind a burning plank. My dad tried to move the flat timber out of the way, but it was too heavy. Nathaniel pleaded for my dad to leave him there behind. Nathaniel was a brave hero. He gave up his life so my dad and Rick could live. I am sure that Nathaniel had a family too, but he gave up everything he had. I still feel for that family, I really do."

The tears stained Karla's sweet face, and she gently rubbed her salty eyes. "Brandy, Rick is my dad. I didn't know that a man gave up his life so my dad could live. Brandy, your dad is Josh, right?"

"Yes, Josh is my dad. I wish I knew who Nathaniel was though. He was such a courageous man. He let my dad and your dad live. I think that would be so hard to give up everything. I wish I had that much courage. In the New Testament, Jesus said, 'Greater love has no one than this, that one lay down his life for his friends' [John 15:13, NASB]."

"What happened to your dad? I mean, why did he quit?" Aimee softly asked, her baby-blue eyes flooding with tears.

"My dad couldn't handle working at the fire station anymore. It killed him to know that Nathaniel had died. He blames himself for not trying harder. He even attempted suicide a year and a half ago, but every time he pulled the trigger, the gun locked. God was totally there that night, preventing him from taking his life in his own hands. The way I see it is that God's not finished with him yet. My dad became a Christian a year ago and completely changed his life. Now my mom is filing for a divorce. She is an alcoholic addict. Pray for me guys. I am losing my family." Brandy whimpered, and she clasped her hand over her mouth as if to keep from screaming. "I am holding onto God. I know he is there for me, but it sometimes is so hard. My family is breaking apart, and I can't do anything about it. All I can do is watch it happen."

"We'll be here for you, Brandy. We promise," Mandy sniffled as the tears continued to descend from her green eyes.

"Can we pray with you?" Tiffany offered.

Nodding her head, Brandy agreed.

"Dear God, we don't understand why Brandy has to go through this. Give her peace in her life as she faces each day. Work in her mom's life. Change her heart from sinful desires, and direct her onto paths of righteousness. Keep her family together. Amen," Tiffany prayed, giving everything over to God. It was a long night as the girls cried themselves to sleep.

The next day unraveled, and Brandy, Tiffany, Karla, and Mandy all woke up in the early dawn of the morning. They had decided the night before to ride up to the lake, which was nearly an hour away. Although Aimee no longer needed crutches, she had chose to stay behind. Besides, she had promised Jesse she would help him stoke out the barn.

As Aimee stroked Diesel's black, shiny mane, she softly asked, "Jesse, didn't you just graduate?"

"Yes, I did. I didn't go to the prom, though. You know I would have taken you if I had," he muttered as he opened Skittles' stall.

Silence reigned for a moment as an unanswered question burned inside Aimee. "Jesse, have you ever heard the story about your dad's accident?"

"Yes, I have. It is so sad. It hurts to even think about it."

"It bothered me all last night. I couldn't sleep very well. I think I know who Nathaniel is."

"Who?" Jesse asked as he shoveled fresh hay into Skittles' stall.

"I think he is—"

Suddenly, a strange tall man with light-blond hair casually entered the stable. As he strode up the hard-packed dirt, he kindly uttered, "Hi, I am sorry to bother you, but I need directions to town. I am not exactly sure which way to go. Actually, I am looking for someone. I have come all the way from California."

Suspicion swept through Jesse like wild fire as he explained to head north. "Who are you looking for anyways? Maybe I could lead you into the right direction."

Introducing himself, the strange man verbalized, "I am James, and I am looking for my aunt, Charlotte Cooper."

Jesse instantly shook his head. "I don't know anybody by that name. Sorry, sir."

"Thank you for the directions to town. I will be on my way. Good day," James pronounced as he strode out of the barn.

As he departed, Aimee gently whispered, "Jesse, I know him. I mean he looks so familiar. I just don't know where I have seen him before." Her mind was boggled as she tried to search through her memory. She didn't recognize the face as much as she did the tender voice. If only she could remember.

California or Edmonton?

When the doorbell rang, Aimee unhurriedly trudged to the front of her aunt's house. Screeching the creaky door open, she slowly glanced up, and to her surprise, the same man who had been at Jesse's a day earlier stood before her.

"Haven't I seen you before?" James paused until he recollected his memory. "Right, now I remember. You were with the kind, young gentleman who gave directions to me the other day."

Smiling with perfection, Aimee sweetly asked, "Can I help you with anything?"

As he stepped inside the air-conditioned abode, he replied, "Why yes you can. Is Charlotte Cooper here?"

Confusion filled Aimee's mind as she scratched the top of her head. "Well, I recall you saying that yesterday, but the only problem is she doesn't live here."

He frowned in frustration. "The Children's Aid Foundation must have given me the wrong name. This is the address they gave me."

It unexpectedly struck her. Perhaps she had seen him before at the orphanage. There were too many people who went in and out of the children's home for her to remember each person in passing. That had to have been how she knew him. Curiosity swirled inside her as she suspiciously uttered, "My aunt, Charlene Carter, lives here. Were you at the orphanage at some point and time?"

"No, I wasn't. If you don't mind, could I speak with Charlene?"

Immediately, Aimee interjected, "Didn't you say at the barn yesterday that you were looking for your aunt? I know you from somewhere. I know I do. Are you my cousin or something?"

Suddenly, Charlene leisurely strolled from the kitchen to where James stood in the entryway.

"Morning, I am James Riley. You probably don't know me, but I am your nephew, Aunt Charlotte." He brushed his thick fingers through his sunlight-blond hair. Aimee instantly glared at him, and he quickly corrected himself as if he covered up his mistake without anyone noticing. "Charlene, of course. Aunt Charlene. Well anyways, I recently received an important letter from the Children's Aid Foundation regarding my younger sister. She is about sixteen or seventeen. The Foundation mentioned that you had a young girl living here with you from the orphanage."

Charlene softly inquired, "Did you just say your last name was Riley?"

"Yes, ma'am, I did." A sunlit smile formed upon his scruffy face.

"I am Aimee Riley," Aimee blurted as a tear slipped down the side of her cheek. How could anyone not have told her that she had a brother? All this time she thought she had no siblings.

"Do come inside. I'll make some coffee," Charlene proposed.

Shyly, he asked, "Do you mind if my wife comes inside? She is just outside in the car."

While Charlene busied herself preparing the coffee, James brought his wife inside.

"This is my wife, Victoria."

Victoria had golden-brown hair and greenish-blue eyes that glistened from the sun that overflowed from the windows. She was wearing dark-blue jeans and a light-pink blouse, which complimented her slim figure quite nicely.

As Victoria stepped into the average-sized kitchen, a tiny figure scurried from behind her. "Hi, evee-body. Where Aimee? Where my auntie? My name Christian, and I two yea old."

Christian was a bigger built boy with light-auburn hair, and his eyes were the color of a sea ocean blue. He was way too cute.

Not only was Aimee a sister, but she was an auntie too. How exciting!

As the adults chatted intently, Christian rolled his trucks and cars across the glossy hardwood floor. Quickly, Charlene poured the fresh dark roast coffee as they sat around the wooden table.

"How come I never knew I had a brother?" Aimee pleadingly asked.

"I was fifteen when you were born. When you were four years of age, I decided to go to college and begin my life. The year after I left I was involved in a serious car accident. It was like God was trying to get my attention because I was the only survivor. I completely devoted my life to Christ. From the accident reports, Mom and Dad must have assumed that I had died. I guess they thought it would be best if you didn't know about me," James presumed, his eyes locking with Aimee's.

"I knew I knew you. I vaguely remember you, but I definitely recognized your sweet, gentle voice. It is shocking. I can't believe I have a brother," Aimee exclaimed.

"Well, you have definitely changed, Aimee," he paused as he sipped his hot cup of coffee. After a moment of solitude, James continued, "I think you are old enough now and should know how Dad died. He was working on a project for the city. Do you remember Dad's profession?"

Aimee could tell it was especially hard for James to share the tragic story as he tried to refrain the streaming tears from escaping from the corner of his eyes. "Yes, he was a roofer."

"In New Brunswick where we used to live, the Mallard Hotel was in the process of being completed. Dad signed a contract with the city and was expected to shingle the roof over a certain period of time. After three months of labor, Dad was almost finished. As he laid down the last sheet of shingles on a steep part of the roof, his harness ripped, and he slid off the building. There was no chance of him surviving."

The pain in his voice echoed as a tear descended softly from his bright-blue eyes. "I wish I could have been a better brother to you, I really do. After Dad died, Mom became addicted to drugs and alcohol. She did it to keep her going through life. After an overdose, she died a sudden, horrible death."

Most of the time while Aimee's mother was alive, she had left Aimee, at age six, all alone in their small house. She had just been trying to survive the terrifying days ahead without her husband. However in doing so, she had abandoned her infant daughter. How could anyone leave a child to defend for him or herself? Who could be so cruel to think of only themselves? Fury and rage burned inside Aimee as she remembered the long, cold nights she had spent by herself. They were awful memories, truly awful, and she only wished she could forget them.

As the foursome chatted, a baby began whimpering. Excusing herself from the table, Charlene quickly waltzed into her bedroom where Mira panted helplessly. Gently, she picked her up and carried her into the yellow kitchen.

Breaking the stiff silence, Charlene rapidly asked, "Would anyone like to hold her? Her name is Miracle, but we call her Mira for short."

Victoria nodded as Charlene placed Mira in her arms. "I remember when Christian was this little. The days flew by so fast. Actually, I am expecting again, and I am due in five months. Your little girl is as cute as a button." A moment of silence stung the misty air before she continued, "We heard about your husband. We are so sorry, Charlene."

Charlene thanked her for being so thoughtful, and she gently replied, "All we can do is pray. The rest is in God's hands."

Victoria smiled and nodded her approval. "Will do."

Finally, James brought up an unexpected topic. With precise words, he said, "Aimee, you don't have to, but I want to invite you to come and live with us back in California. I want to make it up to you for not being the brother you deserved. This is totally your decision." A sly smile crept up on his scruffy face and a loud laugh boomed in the air. "Or you could just stay here with my favorite aunt." The humor reflected in his voice. Everyone was well aware that this was the first time he had been introduced to Charlene.

"James, you'll always be my brother, and it has felt like I've known you my entire life. I have always wanted a brother or sister, and now I do. But if it is okay with you, could I have some time to think on it. If I do come back with you to California, I would love to at least stay here for Mira's first birthday. She's been my sister for almost a year, and her birthday is only a month and a half away. It would mean the world to me."

As a grin spread across his pudgy face, he shyly wondered, "Aunt Charlene, do you mind if Victoria and I stay here with Aimee for the time being. After Mira's birthday, we will be on our way back to California."

"Of course. You are welcome here anytime for as long as you want."

"Sounds like a deal," James blurted.

Everyday that unhurriedly passed, Aimee wished wholeheartedly that James would have been there for her while she was growing up. Although she met him only a week ago, she felt like she had known him forever. She just wished that he had only been a few years older than her and not almost a whole generation. He was practically as old as Charlene was. Five years was about the age gap between the aunt and nephew relationship; it was kind ofweird.

On Friday night, Aimee quickly latched the diamond necklace that Jesse had given to her on her birthday around her neck. Jesse had phoned the night before, and they were planning on going for a walk in the cloudless park nearby.

When the doorbell continuously rang, Aimee scurried to answer it. Swiftly, she grabbed a light jacket and rushed out the door.

The evening June breeze lightly cradled her sweet face, and the sun was beginning to set as the painted sky reflected a colorful rosy pink. Tenseness clung to Aimee's soul, and Jesse immediately noticed she was on edge.

Sincerity filled his heart as he gently asked, "Aimee, is everything all right?"

She cried her heart's desire as he embraced her. "No, I don't know what to do. I have a huge problem, and I don't know how to fix it. I have asked God to show me the right direction, but everyday flies by with no answers, only more questions." As the salty tears tingled down her serene, angelic face, she searched for the right words to say. Finally, she murmured, "I might be moving to California. I just don't know what to do. I'll miss you so much."

Tears clouded his piercing chocolate-brown eyes. He gently ran his fingers through her blond hair and delicately stroked her face. "You can't. You are the best thing that has ever happened to me. I love you, Aimee Riley."

As the tears crawled down his handsome face, she felt tears bubbling up inside her. He had never told her that he loved her before. At least she never knew he had.

Happy Birthday!

As the rain tinkled against the glass windows, Charlene awoke startled at the heartbreaking sound of Mira crying. Lying in the thick, solid wood crib, Mira squirmed uncontrollably as she panted for in-between breaths. Quickly, Charlene lifted her out and held her tightly to her chest as she walked into the kitchen. Victoria was sitting down at the table drinking a cup of hot chocolate when Charlene sauntered in.

"Good morning, Victoria. How did you sleep?"

The young woman appeared restless as she stared blankly into the sunshine that beamed through the large windows. As she turned, the light flickered across her angelic face, and it instantly became apparent that dried tears stained her eyes. What was wrong?

"Is everything all right, Victoria? Are you okay?" Charlene asked, noticing the woman's distress.

Blinking back the continuous tears, Victoria sniffled as she pulled back her golden-brown hair into a ponytail. Finally, she managed to control her unwinding emotions as she replied, "James is gone. He outright left this morning, and he didn't sound like himself. He told me he didn't know when he was coming back."

"Did you get into a fight at all?" Charlene wondered.

Like the soft sun shower outside, the tears continuously leaked from Victoria's bluish-green eyes as she muttered, "No. That's what is so strange about the entire event. He woke up at four this morning and left in a frantic. And to make matters worse, it is our anniversary today. I don't know what is wrong with him."

Charlene hugged the young woman as she tried to calm her down. "Well, maybe he…" her voice trailed off as she tried to think of a possible solution to Victoria's problem. "Maybe he forgot he had to work today. You know, he got that part-time job at the lumberyard for the short time that you are staying here."

"No, he seemed really off edge. He would have told me if he had to work." Victoria glanced down at the rich oak table before her. "Everything seems like it is going wrong in my life, twisting and turning in every direction."

Panicking, Charlene changed the conversation to a more heartwarming topic. "I was wondering if you would like to help me arrange Mira's birthday party. My mom and dad are planning on arriving in three days."

Swiftly, Victoria wiped her face with the soft tissue she clenched tightly in her hand. "I would love to."

For the morning hours of the day, the two ladies chatted about party preparations, which included whether the gathering should be held outside or inside. Obviously it would depend on the weather forecast for that day. While the women were talking, Aimee casually strutted out of her bedroom and into the warm kitchen. "Morning, Mom and Sis. I overheard you guys talking from my bedroom. Can I help with Mira's party?"

"Of course, Aimee, dear," Charlene exuberantly replied.

After an hour, little Christian strode up the wide stairs that led down to the basement. "I thought eveebody had weft me oll aone. I lay in my bed for bout n hour, and then I come up here and then eveebody here." The dramatic changes in his voice and facial expressions created a burst of laughter around the table. "I go play now." Slowly, the little guy sat on the floor and raced his cars in silence.

While everybody was caught up in their conversation, Christian sneakily slid one of his racecars on top of the beautiful glass coffee table in the living room. Rapidly, he pushed the miniature vehicle, and it instantly collided into the angelic figure that gracefully stood on the glass table. Tears stung Christian's bright-blue eyes, and Victoria scurried to comfort him.

"I didn't mean to knock de angel oer. I was just playing."

Charlene quickly skimmed over the angel that Marcy had bought for her. The verse engraved on the angel rang inside her head. "I can do all things through Christ who strengthens me" (Philippians 4:13, NIV). She could do this. She could get through this depression without Todd with the help and guidance of God. He would be her comforter, and he would also be Victoria's during this troubling time.

Suddenly, Charlene realized that Victoria was feeling somewhat of the same loneliness that she was. Todd was not there for Charlene, and right now, James was not there for Victoria. How could James out rightly leave his beloved wife alone with a son and another baby on the way? The emotions Victoria experienced were the exact same ones that Charlene had felt when Todd had been in his accident. Indeed it was a reassurance to know that although they both felt alone, God would be there for them no matter what.

The day seemed like it dragged on forever as Victoria paced back and forth in front of the large window that overlooked the front yard. When she heard a vehicle screech up onto the driveway, she creaked the front door slightly open. To her surprise, James ran up the pathway and held her tightly in his muscular embrace.

"Surprise. Happy tenth anniversary, honey! I love you," James shouted aloud. After he gently kissed her, he slowly went down on one knee. A sly grin shone upon his face as he pulled out a black velvet box from his pocket. "It's for you, Vicki. I love you, sweetheart." Instantaneously, he noticed that Victoria's eyes were swollen and red, and in an apologetic way, he caressed her face in his big hands. "I'm sorry I left this morning. I completely forgot to buy you an anniversary present, and I spent all day looking for the perfect gift to get you. That is why I left in a panic. I didn't mean to scare you."

"I thought you were leaving me. I was so worried." Tears fogged her beautiful eyes.

"I love you, Vicki. I would never even think about leaving you. I made a vow on our wedding day, and as I promised then, I promise now to love you the rest of my life. You are everything to me. I am so sorry I frightened you."

As James gently slid the diamond ring on Victoria's tiny finger, she softly whispered in his ear, "I am just so relieved. I love you so much, James Riley. You are the sweetest and most tender man I have ever met."

"I love you too, Vicki."

Finally, it was the eighteenth of August, and at four o'clock in the afternoon, a vehicle rolled up onto the driveway.

"Papa and Grama here, Mommy. They here already," Mira declared as a vivid smile glittered across her face.

After her grandparents brought in their suitcases, Mira waddled toward them. "Papa and Grama, I one. It my birthday today."

Suddenly, the little girl saw a strange figure through the glass window. "Who is that?"

As the rich, sweet ring of the doorbell chimed, Charlene rapidly opened the rustic, creaky door. "Jesse, I'm glad you came. Aimee told me she invited you. Come on in," Charlene said as she stepped out of the way.

His mouth dropped wide open as Aimee waltzed into the front entry. Her hair was partially pinned back and was styled in tight ringlets. Her baby-blue eyes sparkled as they locked with Jesse's. She looked absolutely stunning.

As they walked into the light-yellow kitchen for supper, he softly whispered, "You look amazing, princess. You are absolutely beautiful." She smiled as she took a seat.

After everyone was squished around the table, Christian politely stated, "I'm going to say the blessing." He bowed his head and folded his chubby hands. "God, thanks for this food. Amen." Rapidly, he chomped into his hamburger patty.

When everybody was decidedly stuffed, Charlene brought out a homemade chocolate cake for dessert.

"Make a wish, Mira," her grandpa urged.

"God, I wish tat my dada be here. Wet him wake up soon. Tank you," she whispered softly as she blew out the tiny flames on the candles.

"Mira, you have one boyfriend," Aimee declared. There was one candle still burning brightly.

"What's a bofend?" Mira curiously asked.

"I'll be your boyfriend," Christian pronounced. "Whatever it is."

Mira agreed as she immediately stuffed her small hands into the chocolate cake that lay before her.

After Aimee finished her dessert, Jesse contentedly asked her, "Do you want to go for a walk, princess?"

"I would love to. I'll ask my mom to make sure that it is okay," Aimee replied.

Quietly, she walked around the oak table and gently whispered in her mother's ear, "Would it be all right if Jesse and I go for a walk?"

The two of them reminded Charlene so much of her and Nate. It seemed like only yesterday when Nate had swept her off her feet. Charlene tried to forget the piercing thought. It had been extremely difficult for her to even read the letter he had given her. "Yes, that is perfectly fine with me."

Slamming the door behind them, Jesse and Aimee leisurely walked down the front steps of the old-fashioned home.

As they ambled down the sidewalk, a light, cold breeze occupied the thick air. Jesse quickly slipped his black jacket off and delicately laid it around Aimee's shoulders. She thanked him as the warmth of his coat took the edge of the chill away.

After ten minutes of stale silence, Aimee sincerely said, "Jesse, I don't know if I should go with my brother back to California. I mean, I love it here, and I have made so many strong Christian friends. I know I am going to miss it here, and even more, I am going to miss you."

He slipped his strong hand in hers to comfort her as the tears gracefully fell from her serene face.

In a deep, clear voice, he slowly answered, "More than anything, I want you to stay here, but I also want you to know that it is your choice. I can't be the one to make it for you. My prayer is that God will lead you to where he wants you to be, whether that is here or in California." He paused as he tried to find the right words. "No matter what you decide, princess, I will wait for you. Even if it is my entire life, I'll wait. You mean so much to me. I wouldn't want to spend the rest of my life with anybody else, but you. I love you, Aimee Riley. I always will."

After a long moment of silence, Aimee calmly murmured, "Jesse, I know I have never told you this, but I love you." As the words tumbled from her mouth, she knew that he was the reason that she couldn't make a complete, straightforward decision.

A tear descended his cheek, and he gazed into her deep blue eyes. "You love me?"

"I love you, Jesse, more than anything. I will wait for you always. You truly are a rare and precious jewel." God's presence filled them completely as they strolled back to the house in silence, hand in hand.

Aimee had to make a definite conclusion whether it was to stay or to go. All she knew was that she had to make it before tomorrow because her brother and sister-in-law had arranged to leave for California in the morning.

Praying softly as she climbed inside her warm bed, she whispered, "God, direct me and help me to make the right decision. I am not sure whether you want me to go or to stay, but I pray that you'd lead me to where you want me to be. I want to thank you, God, for touching my life with a miracle and that miracle being you, Jesus. You have healed me with your love, and I want to give my life back to you. Whatever you need me to do, let me do it for the glory of you. Amen."

Home Sweet Home

The morning unraveled ever so quickly, and as the sun glistened through Aimee's bedroom window, she quickly awoke and rolled out of bed. Unhurriedly, she sauntered into the quiet kitchen where she found everyone sitting at the table eating store bought waffles. Swiftly, Aimee sat down next to her mother, and everyone immediately stopped as they watched her with anticipation.

"Have you decided, kiddo?" James briefly asked.

Slowly, Aimee murmured, trying to hold back the tears, "Mom, I have decided to move to California and live with James and Victoria. It has been a very difficult decision, but I believe that God is leading me to go there. I have prayed about it, and I feel God tugging on my heart. I promise I'll come visit you and Mira soon."

"What bout Jesse? You ove him," Mira's tender little voice reflected her sadness. "I miss you, Aimee."

"I already called Jesse. He knows. I'm going to miss you too, Mira," Aimee softly cried as she swooped Miracle in her arms. "You take good care of Mom. She is going to need you."

"I will, I promise."

All of a sudden, Charlene could not control herself, and the tears that stung behind her eyelids softly fell down her face. Aimee was a daughter to her, and now the seventeen-year-old girl who had taken such a special place in her heart was leaving for good.

"I'll miss you very much, Aimee," Charlene uttered as she dabbed her watery eyes.

"I'll miss you too, Mom. It will be okay. I am sure you will get use to me not being here."

After breakfast, James hurriedly packed all the suitcases in the back of his black Dodge Dakota. Squishing Aimee's brown bag inside, James promptly slammed the tailgate. "We are all set to go. Thank you so much, Aunt Charlene, for everything," he declared as he quickly hugged her good-bye.

"You are welcome, James. Visit soon. Victoria, you take care of yourself. I will definitely be praying for you and the baby," Charlene sweetly murmured.

When Jesse finally arrived in his blue beat-up truck, Aimee ran to meet his welcoming embrace. Oh, how she would miss him. Leaning her head against his chest, she instantly felt the hot tears burning behind her eyes, and unable to refrain them, she let the salty droplets soak into his grey t-shirt.

Slowly, she whispered in his ear, "Jesse, just don't you forget me now. I love you."

A smile shone upon his handsome face. "I won't forget you, Aimee Riley. I promised I would wait for you, and that is exactly what I am going to do. You are worth waiting my whole life for. Just come and visit real soon. I love you, princess."

It would be a new life to adjust to, but she was ready to face the numerous challenges that lay ahead. As she slipped into the back seat of James' truck, James rigged up the engine. Suddenly, a white mini van screeched to a complete stop in front of the antique home, and Brandy, Tiffany, Karla, and Mandy quickly shuffled out.

On impulse, Aimee hopped out of the truck and ran toward them. "Bye you guys."

"Let me quickly snap a picture of you two." Karla motioned for Jesse and Aimee to move closer together. After the photograph was taken, Karla embraced Aimee tightly. "See you soon."

"Miss you, Aimee," Tiffany shouted as Aimee climbed back inside the Dodge Dakota. "Come visit us soon!"

As the vehicle disappeared into the distance, Jesse placed his rough hands in his jean pockets as he whispered under his breath, "I love you, princess."

It was a long drive way to California, and to make the hours pass quicker, Aimee rapidly grabbed her digital camera from her pink purse and captured pictures of the beautiful scenery outside the car window. The trees swayed gracefully on the mountainside, and as the sun gently kissed the ground, it was as if God was embracing the world with his bountiful love.

Finally the extended trip, which took a couple of days, ended as the Dodge crept up in front of the large Californian house. Realizing where she was, Aimee slowly breathed in the San Diego air as she forced herself up the concrete steps. After Victoria unlocked the beautiful maple door, she guided Aimee up a flight of stairs to a huge bedroom. "This is your room. I hope it's okay."

Grateful to her sister for her hospitality, Aimee thanked her as she dropped her bags on the floor and dove onto the small single bed. The room in itself was much more spacious than the one she had stayed in at her aunt Charlene's, but it just didn't have the same feeling of home. Decidedly she unpacked her belongings, and as she carefully placed her clothes inside the dresser drawer, she noticed her brown photo album lying at the bottom of her suitcase. Grabbing it, she flipped through the pages, and as a tear trickled from her baby-blue eyes, she paused to examine a picture of her mom, Mira, and herself sitting next to her uncle Todd in the hospital. Wasn't he one of the reasons she had stayed with her aunt in the first place? Why had she left with her brother now? There was no way of knowing for sure if her uncle Todd would survive his awful coma. He was a dad to her, and she had just left him.

She tossed the album onto the bed and sprinted downstairs to find her brother. He was sitting on the floor in the living room, racing miniature cars with Christian. "James, I have to go home. I just realized that God wants me to be with Auntie Charlene. She especially needs me right now with all that has happened. I don't know why I left her. I promise I will write and keep in touch, but you have to understand that I belong in Edmonton with all my friends and family. I am so sorry, but I know that God is leading me to be there. It is where he needs me."

An enormous grin lit up his face like a bonfire in the middle of spring as he said, "I'll take you back to live with Aunt Charlotte or as you prefer, Aunt Charlene. I'll fly home with you tomorrow, kiddo."

She knelt on the floor next to him and hugged him tightly. "Thank you, James. It means the world to me."

Early the next morning, they boarded the plane. Silence occupied the August air as Aimee gazed out the window. The vastness before her portrayed God's never ending beauty. God was definitely real. He showed his merciful love and grace to all even though no one deserved it. He sent his only Son to die on the cross to pay for each man's sin. He was mighty and great, yet some people were too proud or stubborn to believe in him.

Finally James spoke, breaking the silence that filled the space between them. "You know what, Aimee? You remind me so much of Mom before Dad died. It's unbelievable. The way you and Mom change your mind, it drove dad crazy. And when you smile, you make people feel the way Mom did, warm and free. You have her soft baby-blue eyes that glow when the sun shines down. I know she would be so proud of you, Aimee. Just look at the way you've grown into a beautiful, young, godly woman."

"You really think so?" Aimee paused a moment as she closed her eyes. "James, I wish I could have gotten to know you better when we were younger. It truly does seem like you've been my brother forever."

"Well, that is because I have been, just not in the sense where we've shared a bonding brother-and-sister relationship. I remember when you were a little girl. You always tried to make people smile."

"I did? Well, I don't think I have that unique quality anymore, although I wish I still did."

He smiled as he shook his head. "You have no idea, Aimee. You have no idea."

When the aircraft landed, they claimed their baggage and immediately waved down a taxi. Although it was only about ten minutes to their aunt's house, the drive seemed like it dragged on forever. Finally the cab slowly pulled up in front of the small house, and Aimee swiftly jumped out and skipped up the steps leading to the front door. Quickly, she slid her key into the small opening and unlocked it. "I'm home. I am here to stay!" she hollered loudly.

There was no answer, only the cool summer breeze flooding through the open door. Reacting to the peculiar situation, Aimee decided to call her aunt's cell. After dialing the number, her aunt immediately answered.

"Hi, Mom, it's me, Aimee. I couldn't handle being in California. I know God wants me to be here in Edmonton. This morning James and I caught an early flight out, so here I am at home. I missed you so much."

"Oh, Aimee. I am so glad that you are here to stay. We have missed you too."

There was a long silence that reigned, and as Aimee built up her courage, she nervously asked, "Is everything all right? What's wrong?" She could hear her mother's ailing cry in the background, and she couldn't help but assume the worst.

"Dear, Jesse has been in a dreadful accident. We are at the hospital right now. I am so sorry."

Sprinting back outside in a hurry, Aimee screamed in terror. She felt like she had just lost her most beloved friend. Letting the tears stream down her face, she quickly darted outside and found James unloading their luggage from the back of the cab.

"James, we have to go to the hospital. Jesse is dying, and I don't want to lose him. I love him."

She and James immediately climbed back inside the taxi, and the driver shifted the car into gear. As he pressed harshly on the gas pedal, the vehicle jerked forward and zoomed down the street. In every waking moment, Aimee prayed as the tears endlessly fell from her bloodshot eyes. God would protect him. She just had to have faith that he would.

Upon arriving at the hospital, Aimee and James darted through the chaotic halls and up several winding flights of stairs. As they scurried into the waiting room, Aimee noticed her mother's distress. Karla was sitting next to Charlene, holding Mira who was fast asleep. Rick and Marcy paced the floor while Charlene's parents tried to comfort them.

"What's wrong? Would someone please tell me what happened?" Aimee nervously requested.

Marcy calmly walked toward Aimee as she quickly wiped away the overflowing tears. "Jesse was replacing a bundle of shingles on our barn roof this morning, and he slipped and fell off. The barbwire fence below stabbed his arm. He doesn't have his tetanus shot up-to-date, and Dr. Jens said it was very serious. It is a very infectious virus. Nobody can be sure that he will live. Just pray, Aimee. Just pray. God knows, and we have to trust him."

Suddenly Dr. Jens urgently marched into the quiet, anxious room. "Jesse said that he would not have the procedure performed until he speaks with Aimee's brother, whoever that is. We tried to strap him down, but he ran down the hall. Patients! Anyways, I have made an agreement with him. Is James here?"

"I am James."

Hurriedly, James followed Dr. Jens down the hall.

When Jesse saw James, he slowly asked, gasping for breaths, "James, I would ask Todd this, but he isn't on speaking terms at the moment. I want to ask your permission to marry Aimee if I survive the surgery. I know this is bad timing, but I need to know. As long as I live, I promise I will take care of her. I love her. I would rather die knowing I could have married her than not knowing at all."

When Jesse began breathing hastily, James quickly said, "Yes, you have my permission. I will be praying for you."

"Thank you," Jesse mumbled as the nurses rolled him away. Slowly, James walked back into the dreary waiting room.

Clenching her grandma's hand in her own, Aimee dried her teary eyes. Her grandma squeezed her hand, and it was reassuring to know that she was not alone. "Aimee, I know you aren't my real granddaughter, but I have always had a special place for you in my heart. You are just as important to me as Miracle and Alyssa. You three are my angels."

"You are my very first grandma. You mean so much to me too. I love you, Grandma."

"I love you too, dear. 'God is our refuge and strength, a very present help in trouble' [Psalms 46:1, NASB]. Your mother Charlene kept reminding me about this verse when your grandpa had his heart attack nearly three years ago. Let God help you, Aimee. Let him be your strength. He wants to help you."

"Thank you, Grandma. I needed to hear that right now."

Aimee repeated the verse over and over again as she waited helplessly with everyone else. Praying endlessly, Aimee relied on God through the waiting period as she focused her thoughts and mind upon him. While she was waiting, she realized that she needed Jesus more than she ever knew. He was here for her, sitting next to her and telling her it was going to be all right no matter what the outcome would be.

Having the loss of both parents overwhelmed her continuously, and she could not bear to lose the young man she dearly loved. She had no doubts at all in her mind; she was in love with Jesse Stanford.

The Gift

The weeks slowly passed, and Jesse was continuously gaining strength. Thankfully, Dr. Jens had been able to clean out the toxins from the rusty wires and dress the wound on his arm. Everyone was grateful to God for saving the young boy's life. There was a reason and a special purpose for his life; God wasn't finished with him yet. A few days after the terrifying trauma, James had flown back to California to resume his work and to return to his family. He stayed only as time permitted him to do so in order to ensure Jesse was all right.

As the month of October unfolded, the leaves gracefully fell from the treetops. Fall was here, and the fresh breeze continued to thicken with the arrival of each new day.

"Aimee, are you ready to go? I have Mira's jacket on, and the Durango is heating up outside," Charlene hollered as she quickly tied Mira's tiny runners.

"I'll be right there." Aimee rapidly clasped the diamond necklace around her neck as she scurried out of her bedroom.

Swiftly, Charlene closed the front door while Aimee buckled Mira in her car seat. After everyone was seat belted in, Charlene shifted the car into gear. The drive to the Stanford's house seemed longer than usual. However, it was probably due to the fact that the sun was hiding its radiant face behind the clouds, giving the day a restless and dreary feel.

As the tires padded across the gravel, Charlene slowly eased off the gas and set the gear into park. Swiftly they climbed out of the vehicle, and Charlene promptly carried Mira inside Marcy's warm, cozy house. Meanwhile, Aimee bustled toward Jesse who was sitting peacefully on the hillside.

When she caught a glimpse of his arm in a light-green cast, she sweetly asked, "How are you doing? I have been praying for you. I am so glad that you are all right. I was so worried about you."

A smile lit his face like the twinkling stars in the evening sky. "I am doing much better, especially now that you are staying in Edmonton for good."

Curiosity churned within her as she lowered herself down next to him. "Jesse, how did you fall off the barn?"

As he glanced off into the distance where horses stood grazing in the fields, he softly replied, "I was so torn a part that you had gone to live in California. It was like somebody had ripped my heart out, threw it on the ground, and trampled over it a thousand times. It felt as though you had abandoned me for somebody else. I missed your company and your bright smile. When you smile, it makes my heart soar. It's like you can see right through me. Even though we promised we would wait for each other, I couldn't help but think that in time we both would change. It is a part of life, you know. The tenseness inside me was so fierce that I wasn't paying attention to my work. I thought I had lost you forever, and in my absent-mindedness, I lost my balance and slipped."

The tears gently fell from her baby-blue eyes. He loved her that much? "I am so sorry, Jesse. I promise I won't leave you again. I am just glad that you are okay."

Slowly he lifted himself off the hard-dirt ground and grabbed her hand. "I want to show you something."

As they walked down the hill and toward the stable, he held her hand tightly in his firm grip. Entering the barn, Jesse led

Aimee directly to Diesel's stall. "I want to give Diesel to you, Aimee. Diesel can stay here, and whenever you want, you can come ride him. He is yours to keep."

Embracing Jesse securely, she quietly muttered, "Thank you, Jesse. He is beautiful."

His face softened as he squeezed her hand. "You're welcome. I love you, princess."

"I love you too."

Carefully, Charlene picked Mira up off the floor and held her closely against her chest. "We should be going. Thank you, Marcy, for everything. It was so good to catch up."

"Yes, I haven't been able to talk to you for quite some time."

Suddenly the front door slammed shut, and Jesse and Aimee appeared in the kitchen.

"What happened? You two must be freezing," Marcy declared.

The two stood there drenched from the cold rain outside.

"We ran back from the stable as soon as the rain began, but as you can see, we are all wet," Aimee giggled.

Rapidly, Marcy scurried to retrieve blankets from the closet in the hall. "Here you two go. Now go sit by the fireplace in the living room and warm up," Marcy instructed as she handed them each a blanket. "I'll go make some hot cocoa. Charlene, would you like some tea?"

Charlene nodded as she heard a continuous buzzing sound. As she flicked her cell phone open, she noticed she had a message.

"Hi, Auntie Charlene, Aimee, and Mira, this is James. I just wanted to let you know that we have a bit of a situation. Victoria went to the hospital last night because she could not feel the baby move. Please pray for a miracle. The doctors aren't sure what is going on. God is capable of anything so please pray for us and especially for the little one. I've got to go, but I just wanted to let you know what's happening on our end of the world. I will call you guys later to give you an update. Love you all. Bye."

"Oh no! My nephew left a message on my cell. His wife, Victoria, was rushed to the hospital because she couldn't feel the baby move," Charlene worriedly explained.

As Marcy sat down at the table, she quietly murmured, "Why don't we pray?"

They bowed their heads, and Marcy softly murmured, "God, be with James and Victoria. We don't know why we suffer through these things, but we do know that we are not alone. Be with them, and comfort them as they struggle through this. Please provide a miracle so the dear little baby inside Victoria may live. Bless them this day with the precious gift of a child. Amen."

The night was restless as Charlene and Aimee waited impatiently for James to call. Finally, at two o'clock in the morning, the phone abruptly rang. Racing to answer it, Aimee picked up the receiver. "Hello, James, is that you?"

"Yes it is. Aimee, you are an aunt to a beautiful and healthy girl. Her name is Grace Victoria Riley. Praise God that she is all right. He definitely performed a miracle."

After talking to her brother for a while, she finally hung up and spread the wonderful news to her tired aunt who could barely keep her strained eyes open.

Thanking God as she climbed into her cozy, welcoming bed, Aimee prayed, "God, thank you for everything. You are definitely an awesome, miraculous God. There is none like you, God. No, there is definitely none like you."

The Secret

As the middle of November neared, the snow sprinkled over the earth like crystal diamonds, layering the earth with a festive, enchanting glow. The eighteenth of November unfolded, and Charlene realized it had been exactly two years since Todd's accident and since she had last been in Todd's most beloved place, his garage.

Slipping out into the backyard while Mira was napping, Charlene halted in front of an enormous white door. Quickly, she unlatched it and crept inside. Darkness filled the quiet structure as she fiddled to find the light switch. In deep searching, she finally managed to flick the light on. Suddenly, she flung her hand over her mouth as she gasped for a breath of air. What had happened?

As tears of sadness and depression overwhelmed her, she rapidly dabbed the corner of her eyes with the back of her hand. Before the tragedy, Todd had used his spare time to paint and fix up the garage. Charlene remembered it so vividly. Every once in a while, she used to bring him a cool glass of lemonade with a plate of freshly baked cookies. However, as she peered at it now, it came as a complete shock to her because the place didn't look fixed up at all. It was in worse condition than ever before.

As she gazed at the devastated scene, it was as if a tornado had swept through the entire building. Glass bottles and cans were scattered on the floor, and a beautiful maple cabinet Todd had made was dented and wrecked. Everything in the garage was in complete ruins. Had there been a robbery?

As she stepped over a broken baseball bat, she glanced down at the floor, and there underneath a chunk of wood lay Todd's to do list. Sitting down on the dusty cement, she gripped the grimy sheet of paper and silently read it to herself.

To finish baby crib:

- Cherry stain
- Sixty-Grit sandpaper
- Two inch screws
- Paintbrush

Holding back the streaming tears that nipped behind her eyes, she focused her attention on a wooden-shaped box in the corner. Swiftly, she stood up and glided her small hand across the cherry-stained crib. Had Todd suspected that she was pregnant all along? Curiosity gurgled inside her like a babbling brook as she spotted a note lying on the dirty concrete floor. Rapidly, she picked it up and breathed in the beautiful words.

My Dearest Charlene,

I just went to buy some more stain to finish the crib. I will be back soon. I love you so much, my dearest.

Love always,
Todd

Reading it over again, she noticed the paper was dated. In the top-right corner, it read November 18, the exact date of Todd's tragic accident. Ever since Todd had lost his job, he had been acting differently and had not been his usual self. Not even once had he told her that he had loved her. Perhaps that was why the small note she now held closely to her heart meant so much to her. It carried hope—hope that amidst trials was love. Although Todd had not spoken verbal words, he had still loved her, and nothing in the world would ever change that.

Observing Todd's black journal lying on the wrecked wooden cabinet, the thoughts of a robbery immediately vanished. Slowly she opened the book that held crisp, thick pages of Todd's personal prayers to God. Dying to know his thoughts, she stared at his handwriting.

> Dear God,
>
> I am having a very difficult time with the aspect of losing my job. It breaks me a part knowing that I cannot provide for my beautiful wife. If only I could tell Charlene the truth and quit hiding all my feelings from her. I was fired because I stood up for what I believed in. I believe in you, God, and always will. But the thought of not having a job right now stings me to the very core because I cannot be a provider. What am I going to do, God? Show me the way. Amen.

It was as if Todd was praying to God right then and there, and she was listening intently as he openly shared his heart with him. Slowly, a tear dripped down her flushed face as she flipped the page and fixed her eyes on Todd's deepest, darkest secrets.

> This is so hard for me, God. I don't understand why you let me lose my job. God, I stood up for you. Why? Why is this so hard for me? My wife is never going to forgive me for everything I have done to her. If something were to hap-

pen to me, I would leave her here with nothing, absolutely nothing. God, help me. Give me the strength and courage I need to battle this. I don't even want to talk to her let alone live with her until I can take the responsibility of sharing the load.

The tears poured out of her heart as she wondered what Todd had been feeling deep inside. What had been spinning through his mind? She wished she would have come in here earlier, and maybe in someway she could have helped him struggle through whatever he was facing. They could have gotten through it together. If only she had known.

God, I would never be able to face my wife again if she ever knew what I did with all our money. You were the one who blessed me with such a good job, and you were the one who kept us going when I lost it. But I ruined everything because I couldn't handle it. God, I am having such an arduous time with this. If Charlene ever found out that I gambled away all our money and destroyed everything in this garage, I don't know what I would do. God, I wish wholeheartedly that I could change what I have done, but the pain is dragging every last breath out of me. God, what am I going to do? Give me courage and guide my way. Amen.

Did she really know Todd as much as she thought she did? Wiping away the continuous tears that overflowed from her heart, she whispered a prayer under her breath, "God, why? Why did Todd not tell me what he was feeling? I can't believe he gambled away all our hard-earned money. When he needed me the most, I wasn't there for him. I don't know what to do. It feels like a heavy burden is being dropped on my shoulders, and I can't carry anything else right now. I have enough to deal with. Help me, God, help me."

She was torn apart, and the only one able to mend her broken heart was God. However, right now, she wasn't exactly sure where her relationship with God was. Even though he had promised he would never forsake her, it felt like he had. When Todd's accident had first occurred, she had felt God's warm hand wrap around hers, comforting and protecting her. Now, she felt empty, completely empty inside.

Missing

The middle of December unraveled, and the snowflakes blanketed the earth with a heavenly glow. Slowly, Charlene began decorating her house. A nativity set was arranged in a neat array on her coffee table, and a nine-foot pine tree stood in the corner of her living room. As Charlene stood back and skimmed over the fine ornamented space, Mira toddled toward her.

"Mama, someting missing. Angel missing."

Gently, Charlene smiled as she swooped Mira in her arms. Delicately, Mira placed the serene angel on top of the thick branch.

"Mama, I know wat I want fer Christmas. I want to meet Dadda."

A layer of tears clouded Charlene's green eyes. Her daughter's wish was the same as her own. Mira didn't desire a doll or a stuffed animal; all she wanted for Christmas was for her daddy to come home. How could Charlene ever measure up to that?

The next morning Charlene unhurriedly prepared herself for the long day ahead. After she finished applying her makeup, she steadily walked toward Mira's crib. Glancing down, Charlene nervously gasped. Where was her sweet baby girl?

"Mira, sweetheart. Where are you? Where could have she gone?"

As she sauntered into the living room, she noticed Mira's little blue runners were no longer sprawled on the front carpet. Glancing upward, she stared at the wide open door, her face as pale as crystal snow. How could have Mira escaped? She was way too tiny to reach the doorknob much less unlock it. Charlene's question was instantly answered when she observed a small plastic stool to the right of the door. How in the world was Charlene ever going to find her baby girl? Worry swept through her like a fierce hurricane as she screamed in anxiety. She had already lost Mira once before at the hospital, and she couldn't bear to lose her again.

"God, what are you doing to me? Where's my baby?"

The shrill cry suddenly awoke Aimee, and she instantly ran to comfort her ailing mother.

"What's wrong? Are you okay, Mom?"

"Mira is gone. She ran away!" Charlene bellowed, her emotions burning with fire.

Rapidly, they scurried outside to Aimee's red Pontiac Sunfire and climbed inside. Steering the old red car along the icy, unsmooth street, they searched recklessly for the little girl.

"God, please be with my Mira. Protect her, Lord, and help me to find her. Amen."

"Mom, it's going to be okay. She is perfectly fine. God has given me a comforting peace. He is with her this very moment. Where else do you think we should look?"

Charlene sniffled as she traced her thoughts. Where would Mira disappear to? Was there someone she wanted to see? Instantaneously, everything pieced together.

"Aimee, I know where she is. She has pleaded with me several times to take her to see her daddy. I haven't gone to visit Todd for about a month now. Mentally, I just couldn't do it. I think Mira is at the hospital."

As Aimee directed her Pontiac into the crowded parking lot, Charlene hopped out and raced through the hospital's entrance.

After climbing up several flights of stairs, she quickly turned the corner and slipped inside Todd's room. Instantaneously, Mira bounced off the bed where her daddy lay peacefully and ran toward her mother's welcoming embrace.

"Mama, I otay. I wit papa. I know he gonna be otay. Jesus sittin' wight next to 'im. He wake up soon. I talk to Jesus, and he told me that everyting is gonna be all right. It be in God's timing, not ours."

"How did you get here, Mira?" Charlene asked, her voice sounding slightly worried.

"I follow an angel," Mira replied.

How could such a small child have so much faith? Tears flooded Charlene's eyes as she knelt down and prayed, "Dear God, thank you that my baby is safe. Please forgive me for believing Satan's lies. You would never forsake me, yet I had little faith in you. I lost hope in you, and I don't deserve your redeeming grace and forgiveness. Forgive me, God, for I am ashamed. My prayer is that you'd give me the faith of a young child. Faith is not a feeling; it's believing when we don't feel anything at all."

Slowly, she stood up and tenderly kissed Todd's forehead. "I love you, Todd."

Wasn't Christmas a time for miracles? It was the time of celebrating Jesus' birth, and when he was born, it was a miracle for all people. God had promised his Son, and his Son was sent to save the crooked and depraved world. Christmas was indeed a time for miracles.

God's Unfolding Wonders

"Thank you, Aimee, for watching Mira while I'm gone. See you tomorrow," Charlene declared as she slipped her winter jacket on.

It was Christmas Eve, and she finally felt she was ready to face Todd. Ever since the incident in the garage, she had evaded the thought of visiting him. She just needed time to get used to what Todd had done. It had been a little over a month since she had last seen him, and she was slowly healing from all the pain he had caused her.

Quietly, Charlene closed the creaky door behind her and scurried to her Durango outside. Lowering herself into the vehicle, she promptly jammed the keys in the ignition, and with her eyes fixed on the road ahead, she directed the car past a row of houses. As she parked her vehicle in the spacious parking lot, she gazed at the fluttering, perfect snowflakes that glittered from the heavens. Swiftly she climbed out and trudged through the thick layers of snow.

Entering the warm, lonely hospital, she slowly waddled up to Todd's room. As she slipped inside the dreary room, she instantly sat down on a chair in the corner. Imperceptibly, she grabbed his sturdy hand. It felt so good to have him close to her.

Bowing her head as everything inside her shattered, she prayed, surrendering her life to God, "Dear God, I come before you, lonely and depressed. I feel as though I abandoned you and let you down. Be merciful to me for my lack of faith in you. Todd may not be here with me right now, but God, you are. I feel alone and dismayed. Fill me up with your undivided love and presence. I surrender my life to you." She paused as she suddenly sensed God's overwhelming love wash over her weary soul. "God, I have forgiven Todd. I love him more than anyone could imagine. Thank you for blessing me with Todd in my life to love and care for me. He means the world to me. Give me the strength to be here with him now. He looks so dead inside, and it hurts me to see him this way. 'The Lord himself goes before you and will be with you; He will never leave you nor forsake you. Do not be afraid; do not be discouraged' (Deuteronomy 31:8, NIV).

"God, I am afraid that Todd may die, but I trust that you will bring me through. I yearn to grow closer to you through this, God, and in the past few years, despite all that has happened, I have felt a renewing peace in my life—and that peace is from you alone, Lord Jesus. God, you have never left me nor forsaken me. Why should I be afraid? I guess it just scares me to think that Todd may leave me when I need him the most. I know I have taken care of Aimee and Mira for a year and a half now, but the salary I make isn't enough. God, if Todd does die, provide me with a suitable job to keep this family going. No matter what happens, I will stay strong in you."

She felt a peace from God sweep over her as she poured out all her confused thoughts. Somehow God would work out everything according to his purpose. She knew one thing for sure. It was a reassurance to know that God would never leave her. She had held onto everything she had left of Todd, but she had to face it, the future may hold him or it may not. "God would be her refuge and strength, a very present help in trouble" (Psalms 46:1, NASB).

Whatever happened, God would always be there for her.

Slowly she rubbed Todd's forehead and stroked his short, crisp blond hair. He would be all right; she just knew it.

For a few moments, Charlene pondered everything that had happened in the past few years. Even if God had taken almost everything from her, he had also richly blessed her. She had faced numerous challenges, yet she knew without a shadow of a doubt that God had been there for her. She didn't always understand his ways nor was she meant to.

Feeling the hurt within her relinquish, she finally was ready to forgive, and as she tenderly rubbed Todd's hand, she softly uttered, "I believe that God has taken me through this journey to focus on him instead of my worldly desires that no longer have a yearning in my soul. God has taught me to love when it is hard to love and to forgive when it is arduous to forgive. Testing me, he has shown me who I really am, and I have had to change. This has been a time of prayer, and I have put my whole trust in God to bring me through. It has not been easy, and I know it is just the beginning of the difficulties that I am going to be challenged with.

"Todd, from the time you lost your job until now, I have loved you, and nothing you do could ever change that. I wish I could have been there for you when you gambled your hurt and pain away. I have already forgiven you for your mistakes and only hope that you will forgive me for mine. I love you, Todd." She paused as she thought about the many blessings God had graciously given her. Tears descended her face as she continuously rubbed his forehead. "You have a beautiful niece who has grown into a wonderful daughter of ours. And you have a precious baby girl who is a year and a half. They miss you, Todd, and they need you. Todd, you must understand I wanted to tell you that I was pregnant before the accident, but I was scared. Maybe if I had told you, none of this would have happened. Maybe you thought I was keeping a secret from you, but that was not my intention at all."

"I already knew, Charlene, that you were pregnant," Todd murmured as he gradually opened his sparkling brown eyes.

As he squeezed her hand, she felt tears brimming her eyelids. Was she imagining something? Was it true? Was he really awake?

"Todd, you are all right! It's a miracle!"

Embracing her, he wrapped his comforting arms around her.

"Thank you, God. Thank you," Charlene whispered joyfully.

For a moment, they held each other close as joyous tears filled their eyes. Charlene couldn't be happier. The man she loved was there with her, not just lying there helplessly but holding her in his firm grasp.

"I was so foolish. I left you here with nothing because I was selfish and confused." Todd became silent as a tear slid from the corner of his eye. "I am so sorry I did this to you. Will you forgive me?"

A light, soft smile formed upon Charlene's face as she replied, "I already have."

It was the best Christmas present Charlene had ever received. She was right. God could perform such a miraculous wonder that seemed most impossible. But with God, nothing was ever impossible.

Reunited

It was a cool, brisk morning, and the snow sheeted the ground with a thick layer of ice. As the sun peeked out from behind the fluffy clouds, tiny, perfect snowflakes gracefully descended from the sky. Slowly Charlene assisted Todd out of the hospital and guided him through the thin fog into the lonely parking lot.

As the car rolled down the bumpy street, the tires suddenly gripped a black sheet of ice. Swiveling uncontrollably, Todd quickly clasped his hand tightly around her shoulder as she quickly corrected the vehicle's path. Abruptly, he closed his eyes and turned his head.

Noticing Todd's rapid gesture, she softly asked, "Are you okay, Todd?"

Shaking continuously, he quivered in pain, "Yes, it just scared me that's all."

Was he still in shock from the accident? The jerking movement caused by the slippery ice must have in the slightest way reminded him of his car collision. Thankfully he seemed to calm down a bit as she regained control over the vehicle and steered it into the clear direction of home.

After she parked the black Durango on the driveway pad, she helped Todd inside the warm, cozy house. Slowly, Charlene screeched the creaky door open. When Aimee saw her uncle limp through the doorway, she bolted toward him. "Uncle Todd, you are alive! I was expecting Auntie Charlene but definitely not you."

"I haven't seen you, Aimee, since you were eight years old. You look so different. How old are you now?"

"I am seventeen. It's so good to see you, Uncle Todd."

"You too, kiddo."

As Mira scuttled toward her daddy, she stared into his deep chocolate eyes. He scooped her up in his arms, and she giggled with joy.

"Hi, Papa. Today Christmas. I opened first pesent aleady."

"What did you get, Mira?" Todd grinned with pride.

"I just got you. I wanted to meet you."

He wiped his teary eyes as he held his daughter in his arms. "You are very special, Miracle. I love you, sunshine."

"I love you too, Papa."

At around one in the afternoon, a brand new silver Rendezvous halted in front of their house, and an elderly couple slowly climbed out. As Charlene's parents entered the old, rustic home, her mother suddenly backed away. A stunned look spread across her wrinkly face. "He's alive. Praise God! Charlene, why didn't you tell us Todd woke up?"

"I didn't have the chance to. He just woke up last night. The doctor ran some tests on him this morning. Everything was fine, but Dr. Jens firmly advised that Todd remain in the hospital's care for at least a week. However, as stubborn as Todd is, he refused. He wanted to be at home for Christmas."

"Well, Todd, it is absolutely wonderful to see you again. How does it feel?"

"It feels like I had a good long sleep. If I'm tired something must be wrong with me. Charlene told me I was in a coma for over two years," Todd laughed.

After the Stanfords arrived ten minutes later, everyone sauntered into the living room. As Marcy sat down on the soft leather couch, she stared at Charlene in confusion. "Charlene, you should have told me you had a brother. I always thought it was just you and Sandra."

Bursting into a roar of laughter, Charlene could not help herself. Instantly Marcy interrupted, an upset tone stinging the edge of her voice, "Well, aren't you going to introduce him?"

"All right, Marcy, I would like you to meet my husband, Todd."

"Whoops! I am so happy for you, Charlene. God is so amazing." Pausing a brief moment, Marcy smiled as she tried to hide her embarrassment. "Todd, you do look a lot different from how I remember you."

Marcy looked as though she was deep in thought as she traced her memory. "Charlene, you married Todd Carter? The Todd Carter? You disliked him so much when we were growing up."

"Yes, I did, but that was because he used to yank on my pigtails in Sunday school class."

Todd abruptly interjected, "Well, let's not forget, Charlene, that you gave me the most attention."

Smiling wildly, Charlene embraced her wonderful husband. It was so good to have him back in her life.

Todd quickly changed the subject as if to direct the conversation to his old friend Rick. "So are you still working at the fire station? My wife told me about your accident."

"Yes, I just started there again about two weeks ago. The accident prevented me from working for a while. You know, my co-worker, Nathaniel, gave up his life for me. I feel horrible taking him away from his family while I am here enjoying mine," Rick uttered as if he were about to cry.

Immediately Charlene fled to her bedroom, tears flooding her eyes, and Marcy swiftly followed her. "What's wrong, Charlene? Are you okay?"

Charlene shook her head, the pain seizing her insides. Comforting her, Marcy gently embraced Charlene who was breaking down into endless sobs.

"Nathaniel…was my first husband. I am sorry, it's just that I was never told how Nate had died except that it was due to a fire incident. It's only been two years and ten months; I am still grieving his loss." She sniffled continuously as she wiped her runny nose with the back of her hand.

"I am so sorry, Charlene. I had no idea Nathaniel was your former husband. I didn't even know you were married before. I guess we lost contact after high school. How long were you and Nate married?"

"Eight years. This year would have been our tenth anniversary."

The room was filled with a quiet silence.

"Charlene, I understand."

"Understand what?"

"Nathaniel's last words. 'I love you, Char. Take care, my beautiful.' He was saying it to you."

The tears began pouring from Charlene's dry eyes as she suddenly remembered the dream she had a day after Todd's accident. It was Nate, not Todd. He had said the exact same words Marcy had just repeated. Oh, how she would miss him.

Suddenly, Todd entered their bedroom as Marcy departed. Charlene was shaking continuously. "Are you okay, honey?" He wrapped his burly arms around her as she buried her face deep in his chest.

As she wiped away the tears, she whispered, "Todd, I love you. Don't ever leave me again. I thank God continuously that you are okay."

"I love you too. You are everything to me, Charlene." Slowly, he kissed her as he tenderly stroked her face. "Let's go visit with our company."

As Aimee sipped her steaming hot chocolate, Jesse glanced at her and stared for a brief moment. The way he looked at her created a burst of butterflies in her stomach, and she quickly turned away, resuming her conversation with Karla.

"I got you something, Karla." Aimee gently placed a large box in her friend's hands. Lifting off the lid, Karla carefully pulled out a brown purse.

"It's beautiful, Aimee. I'll use it everyday. Thank you. Here, this is for you. Tiffany helped me pick it out."

Slowly, Aimee opened up the tiny box and withdrew a blue engraved flower necklace. The tiny letters on the back read Best Friends for Life. A cheerful smile erupted on Karla's cute round face, and her reddish-blond hair shone in the light as she eagerly waited for Aimee's response.

"I love it, Karla. It's absolutely the perfect present. Thank you so much."

Abruptly the doorbell chimed, and Aimee immediately jogged to retrieve it. Welcoming James and Victoria inside, she invited the foursome into the warmth of the living room.

"Hi, Auntie Aimee. I got a new sister, and her name is Grace Victoria Riley," Christian piped up.

Gently, Victoria pulled Grace out of her baby seat and placed her in Aimee's arms. Grace's eyes were almost a rich sky-blue, and her curly blond hair was beginning to take on a shade of auburn.

Tugging on Aimee's dark-blue jeans, Christian bravely shouted, "Is it time to open presents? Hey, Great Aunt Charlene, your angel isn't broken." Slowly he grabbed the angel off the coffee stand and waved it in the air, instantly forgetting his former request. Charlene swiftly snatched the angelic figure out of the little boy's chubby hands and positioned it back onto the glass table.

The little guy appeared to be deep in thought, and he finally stammered, "How bout we open some presents? Sounds good to me, and I know it sounds good to you guys too." He planted himself beside the sweet fragrant pine tree, and everyone gave into his demand.

Christian pointed his finger at Aimee. "You go first, Auntie."

Slowly, Aimee tore off the wrapping paper and delicately pulled out a black velvet jacket. "Grandma and Grandpa, this is beautiful. I love it. Thank you so much."

The aged couple smiled as Aimee slipped it on. "It fits perfectly," Aimee pronounced as she embraced her grandparents.

"My girlfriend goes next. Go ahead, Mira," Christian instructed as he began to tickle her.

"Don't, Christian. That tickles," Mira pouted. As Mira quickly ripped the red paper off the package that held a little doll inside, her face lit up instantly. "It is the best Christmas! Tank ya, Mama and Papa, fer doll and tank you, God, fer lettin' papa wake up. It's a miracle!" Todd held her in his muscular arms as she started giggling.

After everyone finished opening presents, Christian scrunched up his face like a chipmunk. "I'm starving. When are we going to eat?"

"Right away, Christian. The turkey is ready. Everyone can come sit down," Charlene declared. Immediately, everyone huddled around the oak table, and Jesse rapidly squished in next to Aimee.

He leaned close to her and whispered in her ear, "I have something for you. I'll give it to you after supper."

She stared into his deep brown eyes and held his gaze until Todd began praying.

"Thank you, God, for this wonderful meal you have set before us. Bless the hands that have prepared it. Thank you for sending your Son to save us. We celebrate Jesus' wondrous birth as we spend time with one another. Thank you for everything. In Christ's name, I pray. Amen."

The turkey, mashed potatoes, stuffing, and the various arrays of salads were all passed around the table until everyone was satisfied.

As Mira swallowed her last bite of fruit salad, she politely asked, "Mama, can we sing 'Happy Birthday' to Jesus? It be his birthday, right?"

Todd grinned with delight, knowing that Mira was his very own little girl. Joyful tears sprinkled down Charlene's face as she promptly brought a beautiful cake to the table that read Happy Birthday, Jesus!

After Aimee finished gulping down her cake, Jesse tenderly grabbed her hand and pulled her over to the leather couch in the living room. As he bravely handed her his neatly wrapped present, he slowly uttered, "This is the first part of my gift. I hope you like it."

Unwrapping the box, Aimee silently read the tiny note inside.

> *Aimee,*
>
> *I want you to know how much I love you. You mean more to me than any earthly thing. When you look at this, you can always remember how much I really do care for you.*
>
> *Merry Christmas!*
>
> *Love always,*
> *Jesse*

Steamy tears boiled at the corner of her eyes as she tightly held the antique picture frame. She wiped away the tears as she stared continuously at a beautiful portrait of them together in front of her aunt and uncle's house. Engraved words appeared on the side, "I'll always love you, princess!"

"Thank you, Jesse. I will cherish it forever, just like you."

"Karla took the picture of us before you left with your brother to California. I am so glad you came back. You have no idea how much I cried while you were gone. I thought I lost you."

A soft, delicate smile unraveled upon her face as she gently handed him a package from off the maple hardwood floor. "This is for you. Merry Christmas, Jesse!"

As he uncovered a fancy red dress shirt, he grinned with pleasure. "I have always wanted a shirt like this. Thank you, Aimee."

Abruptly, he became tense and uneasy as he nervously pulled a black velvet box from his pocket. "I have wanted to ask you this for a long time." He gently grabbed her hand as he slowly went down on one knee. "Aimee Riley, would you marry me?"

Her face glowed like the angelic figure on the coffee table as if she thought he would never ask. Softly, she smiled. "Yes, I will, Jesse Stanford. I love you."

"I love you too." Slowly, he slid the sparkling diamond ring on her forefinger, and she gazed deeply into his fierce chocolate-brown eyes.

"Aimee, Bandy on phone. It for you," Mira interrupted the romantic, enchanting moment.

Leisurely, Aimee arose from the couch and unhurriedly strutted to the phone.

"Hello."

"Hi, Aimee. It's me, Brandy. Guess what?"

"What?"

"My mom became a Christian last night, and she withdrew the divorce. Thank you for praying. Aimee, I am so excited. I get to spend Christmas with my family, and we are all together again."

"I am so happy for you, Brandy. That is exhilarating news. Thank you for calling."

"Merry Christmas, Aimee."

"Merry Christmas! See you soon."

"Bye."

Sprinting back to the couch, a glorious sensation from God swept over her. Indeed, Christmas was a season for miracles.